# HOLY
# DEATH

Down & Out Books
3959 Van Dyke Rd, Ste. 265
Lutz, FL 33558
www.DownAndOutBooks.com

The characters and events in this book are fictitious. Any similarity to real persons, living or dead, is coincidental and not intended by the author.

Cover design by J.T. Lindroos

ISBN: 1-943402-25-6
ISBN-13: 978-1-943402-25-0

## DEDICATION

I dedicate this book to my friend and one of my favorite novelists, Les Edgerton. He showed up in my life when I wasn't sure why I was doing this writing thing, and he showed me why I should keep going. His books *The Bitch* and *The Rapist* have kicked me into a higher gear, and I'm thankful for his support.

There would not be a fourth Billy Lafitte novel without Les.

Much love, brother.

# CHAPTER ONE

One-thirty in the morning in a truck stop outside of Hattiesburg, Mississippi. A shout of *Goddamn!* from the men's room made everyone turn, forks and mugs frozen in mid-air, until this trucker came out waving his hand in front of his face like whatever it was in there was the stinkingest goddamned thing he'd ever sniffed. Some of the folks in here, mostly men, mostly tired, and mostly white, laughed because they thought he was making a joke about his own shit, right?

But he kept shouting. "Goddamn! Any of you motherfuckers named La Fit? Anyone know what a La Fit is?"

"You mean Lafayette?"

"No, not Lafayette. There's no 'y' in it."

The tall black kid working the flattop said, "Spell it?"

"It's L-A-F-I-T-T-E. That's La Fit."

Kid said, "I think it's La Feet. Like, French or something, know what I'm saying?"

One trucker at the counter said, "Yeah, you're right. It is."

"So what the fuck's a La Feet, then?"

The fat girl pouring coffee said, "Pretty sure it's a pirate. Or a voodoo queen. I forget."

And then there was some babbling about Jean Lafitte versus Marie Laveau and how anyone this close to New Orleans should know the difference, but the first trucker said, "I don't think it's some dead pirate. All I'm saying is someone took a handful of shit, smeared it on the wall in there, saying they're looking for a Lafitte."

"Serious?"

"I'm telling you, I've got to drop one mighty badly, but not in there. Not now. Shit, I'm going to the Arby's down the road." He high-tailed it for the door, dropped his copy of *Cigar Aficionado* on the floor, and let out a bad fart leaning over to get it. Then a grunt and "Sorry. I've got to hurry."

After he was gone, a few guys went and took a look and came out either laughing or shaking their heads, disgusted. They snapped pics of it on their phones and showed them to the guys who didn't want to look and risk losing their greasy breakfasts. The smell, they said. Holy shit, the smell.

The tall black kid working the flattop, called Alonso by the fat waitress, disappeared for a few minutes, then came back with a mop and rolling bucket, cursing under his breath until he reached fever pitch and shouted at the fat waitress "Ain't nobody said nothing about cleaning up people's shit!"

"Just shut up and get it done!"

"Can't it wait until the next shift?"

"You want me to kick your ass then still make you do it?"

"Aw, fuck you, you fat bitch." But he rolled the bucket toward the bathroom anyway.

Inside, there was a short guy looking at the wall. He wore khaki shorts and a pullover polo and cap with the name of the company he drove for—Muscle Max. The smell of the shit was as bad as the other truckers had said, and the texture was nutty, corny, thick. Sure enough, written in three foot-high letters, *WELCOME HOME LAFITTE.*

"Jesus."

The driver said, "Mm hm." Nodded. He had his bottom lip pulled in between his teeth.

"Got to be a crazy motherfucker who did that, you know what I'm saying?"

Shrug.

Alonso pulled the mop up over the bucket, let it drip. The driver didn't move. "You mind? Need to take a picture first?"

The driver shook his head. Rumbled when he spoke. "I'm good."

Before Alonso could say something else, the little truck driver was gone. Alonso got pissed some more. Probably that one there was the guy who done it. Alonso put up the plastic yellow "Slippery" sign with his free hand, right in the middle of the doorway, then slapped the heavy-ass mop against the wall and watched the water run down over the shit, turn brown, and stream toward the floor.

Alonso said, "Shit."


The Muscle Max driver headed back toward his table, the remains of a catfish sandwich and fries on his plate, a half-empty glass of Mr. Pibb beside it. He tossed a twenty down, way too much for what it cost, and walked out without another word. The fat waitress named Melissa noticed. He hadn't been very friendly to her, but not unfriendly either. She thought she had made him all mad, asking him where he was headed, asking if he needed a shower, because, yes, he sure as fuck did. At first Melissa wondered, too, if this was the guy writing in shit, but she was pretty sure he didn't go to the bathroom the whole time until after another one had pointed it out.

Had he been offended because she was flirty? Not that she *was,* because she had a boyfriend, plus the guy's skin color didn't do it for her. She liked them black. Real black. Always had. Her current boyfriend was white, but just because, you know? If she didn't have to be all *proper,* suppose that was the word, she'd go for the chocolate, and she didn't mind if everyone knew it. So bring on judging from other white bitches in school—and black bitches, too—but Melissa was who she was, and her mamma said people are born to like who they liked, and were also born to weigh what they weighed, so if the little truck driver didn't like her *vo-CAB-uh-lary* or her hairstyle or her big hips and big ass, then fuck that prick. Bet he was a racist. I mean, clean-shaven with no sideburns, his face hard as if it had been chewed up by a dog.

Still, he had also left her, like, an eight dollar tip.

She watched him out the window as he headed toward his delivery truck, black with gold letters on the side—Muscle Max, Peoria, Illinois—and a phone number. Melissa didn't know what Muscle Max was, but that's what the guy was driving, matched the shirt and the cap. Wearing shorts, too, tight because the guy had some muscle on him, and black sneakers, ankle socks. He couldn't help what he had to wear to work. It didn't match his chewed-up face. She thought about looking up

Muscle Max later on the internet, but then there were a couple of guys with empty coffee cups, including one fine-looking black man all by himself at a table for the last hour, ordered coffee only, except he'd brought his own bottle of Patron silver along to pour in it. Didn't look like no trucker. If she didn't have a boyfriend at home, this one might have been a good sugar daddy. Sure enough was a Rolex on his wrist and the keys to a Caddy on his table.

"Come on, baby. I see you looking." He waved her over, and when she got there, he wrapped his arm around her giant hips and squeezed her close. He pretended her sweat stink didn't make his coffee and Patron back up into his throat a little bit, and she liked the effort. No way to avoid picking up the stench, not working here.

"The one who left, you didn't happen to get a name, did you?"

She shook her head. "He didn't say much except to order. Did you see which truck he was driving?"

"Yeah, yeah." Another squeeze. "He hasn't been in before, has he?"

"If he was, I don't remember."

"Mind topping off my coffee?"

She did, then pointed at the Patron with the coffee pot. "You going to be okay to drive tonight? If not, I could take you home."

He smiled up at her, teeth like bricks of ice, even after all that coffee. "A fine offer. I appreciate it. I'll let you know."

Melissa smiled back and nibbled her bottom lip and went back behind the counter. When her odor finally cleared the table, he could swallow again and take a nice breath. He picked up his phone, called Lo-Wider, said, "You getting this?"

"I watched him climb up in his truck. I know it's him, man, same one I seen, I know it."

"Positive?"

"What I just say, DeVaughn?"

Okay, yeah, don't micro-manage. DeVaughn said he was sorry and backed off, told Lo-Wider to follow the truck, call back when it stopped.

"Can't Crocker take over, man? We *tired*."

"Don't lose that truck. Bump up more if you got to, but don't lose that fucking truck."

DeVaughn Rose hung up, licked his lips. He took another look at Melissa, who was watching the TV, dead-eyed bored, munching on Funyuns, washing it down with Diet Mountain Dew. Okay, if it was any other night, *any* other night except this one he'd been waiting years for, who knew? Something about this white girl. If he could've got her back to his place, let the bitch take a shower...

...but he was in a good mood. His prey was in the trap. Why shouldn't he enjoy the rest of his evening? If she wanted to get picked up, he'd pick her up. He liked her eyes. He liked her shape.

This Lafitte—the motherfucker who shot his brother—him and that other cop, Paul Asimov, who was already dead, DeVaughn never thought he'd see the day. Really, not until that prison break, never thought he'd see the day. Until a young man named Lo-Wider had called on the way home from his mom's place in Memphis last week and swore, just swore—*Swear. To.*

6

*God. Jesus*—this dude he saw at Waffle House? Dead ringer.

Motherfucker.

So they did a little homework—careful, careful, so Lafitte wouldn't spook like some goddamn deer. Next time he was out on a delivery, DeVaughn had some people watching. Friends, some newbie Black Coast Mobsters he dropped some cash on. The Muscle Max driver was working his way South, for sure. It was a long couple of days, waiting for him to dip down far enough into the Bible Belt for DeVaughn to be sure where Lafitte, if it was him, was going.

It wasn't until Lo-Wider called and said he was on the tail of the Muscle Max truck south of Jackson that DeVaughn decided to get involved in person. Drove up to Hattiesburg, waited for the truck to pass, and got lucky the man needed to stop where he did, right here at this greasy spoon where DeVaughn paid that white beardy trucker hours to do what he did in the bathroom. Call it a homecoming gift. For the first time since it started, DeVaughn had been there, wanting to be absolutely sure, because he hadn't seen Motherfucker in years, and if DeVaughn was going to do what he had been dreaming of doing every night since he saw his brother, unrecognizable, in a body bag after the water and bugs had had their way with him, it had better be the right motherfucker.

"Welcome home, Billy Lafitte." He raised his mug in a mock toast.

Melissa took it as a sign to come fill him up. And this time, her odor was less sweat and more Funyuns. He passed her the key to his Caddy and said, "Ready when you are." She grinned and told him she could leave right now if she wanted, just let her get her purse. DeVaughn was feeling good. As long as his boys were watching over Lafitte's truck, he might as well have some Funyuns tonight with this waitress's big ol' ass, knocking chairs out of her way as she walked back to the counter.

# CHAPTER TWO

When the pain came, it was the hand of Death himself squeezing Lafitte's left shoulder, firing up along his neck, down his arm, and across his chest. Took his breath away so bad he had to pull the truck onto the side of Highway 49. Pain had been chasing him a week now, at first only when he was loading or unloading the truck. Then whenever he walked. And now any old time.

That's what Death had planned for him, right? Let him reach this close to home and then kill him before he got there? Fuck you, Death, you motherfucker. Fuck you.

It gave him another squeeze.

Truth was, Lafitte didn't have a sane reason to go home anymore. Maybe he did back when they had first trapped him, calling him out of hiding from Steel God's biker gang. But then he ended up murdering four people—flat-out murder, not "line of duty" shit like when he'd been a cop. Then he went to prison. All sorts of prices on his head. Someone tried to collect in the middle of a prison riot, blizzard, and power outage all in one. Laffite watched his own son die—only eight years old, visiting with his grandmother, both of them trapped in the riot. He had carried Ham's body out into the snow, climbed over the fence with the boy over his shoulder. After all that, they had tazed Lafitte, then shot him, but Lafitte did what he had to do to live—he dove into the nearest snowbank and dug his ass as far away as he could. No one saw him do it, and the wind erased all traces before they could figure it out. Besides, who the fuck was going to come after him?

Most days now, whenever he woke, be it morning, night, didn't matter anymore, he remembered what it felt like having a gunshot wound and electric shivers while buried in snow, and he wondered why he bothered to fight so hard for his life after all. Jesus, if this was all he had left, if this was all he had to live for...what was "this" anyway?

Except for the letters he had received in prison. They pointed him south. Home.

Billy Lafitte had been a delivery driver for Muscle Max for about four months. Muscle Max sold protein drinks and vitamins and weightlifting equipment and supplies from their base in Peoria, Illinois to franchises throughout most of the Midwest, and even some decent chain grocery stores. He had started at the warehouse, picking up the supplies, driving them to the customers, unloading them, collecting signatures on the invoices. Then he would drive back to Peoria to wait for the next trip.

But he was delivering more than protein drinks and weights and whatnot. There was something else, too. Something that had made Muscle Max a real player a lot faster than its bullshit supplements ever would. Freshly squeezed juice—anabolic steroids, HGH, testosterone. All colors and flavors, ha ha ha.

Can you see it?

Can you see a physically drained and starved Lafitte emerging from six weeks in the frozen woods, GSW barely healed, in stolen clothes paying for a gym membership with a stolen credit card so he could build up some strength?

Can you see Lafitte looking for some sort of job in the paper he'd found left behind at Taco Bell? Can you see him taking handyman jobs for cash until he had enough to buy a beater? Can you see him, week by week, buying better clothes, getting his hair cut, getting a shave from a barbershop with a striped pole and charged twelve bucks?

Can you see him applying for the Muscle Max job after hearing all the rumors around the gym about its real money makers?

What you can see, we know goddamned well, is Lafitte getting back on the juice big time, taking a pay cut to partake, so he could pump his body back in tip top shape faster than if he kept on trying good old-fashioned rest and rehab. The bosses didn't give a shit. Saved them some money, and most of their other drivers had the same deal. It was all good.

Until his heart started trying to murder him.

He held his arms tight, shaking, and let out a wail. His jaw was killing him, too, and he stretched his mouth wide. Hoped it would subside before a state trooper got curious and pulled in behind the truck. He needed to keep driving, make it to a rest area or big parking lot where he could get a little sleep. The pain always went away when he slept. The pills helped, too. Turned out guys who trafficked 'roids also had their hands on some sweet pain meds, but they worked less and less with each handful. Lafitte wondered if they could get him some nitro, maybe. Shouldn't be hard to find, especially not in

America's Deep-Fryer, Mississippi, but he couldn't wander into a drug store and flat-out ask, so there.

To take his mind off the aching, he pulled back onto the road and dialed his boss, who should probably be asleep. Lafitte would leave a voicemail, no biggie. Surprised the hell out of him when the man answered on the second ring. "The fuck are you? I'm this close to calling the cops."

"It's okay. I'll leave the truck somewhere for you. Give me two more days."

"I didn't give you any fucking days. You stole my goddamned truck."

Another wave of pain. He clenched his teeth. "If I was really stealing your truck, I wouldn't be calling you. I had something to take care of."

"Take your own fucking car. Jesus, I can't afford this."

"Two days. I'll be back on the third, or I'll make sure the truck gets back to you. Something I need to take care of."

Quiet on the other end. His boss, a mid-level guy at the warehouse who probably made more off the 'roids than his salary, was pretty pumped himself, but in a glossier way. His was stage-quality muscles. Lafitte couldn't tell if the man had ever even been in a good fight. A real one.

Finally, the boss said, "Who the fuck are you, anyway? I thought I could trust you."

Made Lafitte grin. Lafitte had given him at least three fake names. The boss had never asked for ID. "I don't know what gave you that idea."

"Just...just...give the truck back and I'll keep the law

out of it. Okay? I mean, you're so fucking fired, but let's keep it civil."

"I get it. I really do." Lafitte hadn't really planned on delivering the stash currently squirreled away in the back. It was a *severance package*, yeah. "I'm sorry about this. You've been a good boss, and it's been a good job. But I'm not a good job type of guy."

He hung up and chucked the phone out the window onto the highway. The only reason he'd called the man was to hold off on the cops—the boss wouldn't want them poking around the truck anyway, and Lafitte wasn't in the mood to steal another car right now. Two more days was really all he wanted, so he could do what he had to do, what her letters had asked him to do.

Ginny. The road sign ahead looked like it said "Ginny." His ex-wife's name. Last he had heard, she was in a facility in Mobile, Alabama, locked inside her own head. She could still talk, but only a little, still walk, still enjoy the breeze on her face and her toes when she sat outside, but otherwise she was in a mental bunker of her own design, cut off from the outside world. But the road sign didn't say "Ginny." It said "Gulfport." He wasn't far now from the crossroads where I-10 ran east-west. Lafitte needed to go east. Mobile was another two hours. But not tonight. Not with this sort of pain. He needed his sleeping bag, his Oxy, his locked truck. As he pulled into the glow of the streetlamps at the cloverleaf exit, he had to blink and blink again. Last he'd seen his hometown, it was only a few weeks after Hurricane Katrina. It had been a corpse. It had been knocked back to the goddamned Stone Age. But look at this. *Look* at it! Must be three, four times as much stuff here as there had been before. It was massive—giant shopping center on the left, another on the right, a line of fast food and fast casual joints, signs still blazing.

Gulfport had always been a decent-sized Coast town, but nothing like New Orleans to the west or Mobile to the east. The casinos had started to change the landscape back in the nineties. Lafitte had been sure things would get quieter after a fucking apocalyptic hurricane. Who would want to live through that shit again, right? But he was dead wrong. Not only were they up for another round, but they'd found a whole bunch of idiots willing to move here and take their chances, too. Gambling could do that to people. First it was their paychecks, and before long it was their lives.

Even this early in the morning, hours before dawn, it was still busier than expected, as if the town never slept. The bigger the influence of the casinos, the lesser the pull of the fishing industry, old-fashioned neighborhoods and a good eight hours sleep. Lafitte looked at the dashboard clock. Maybe he could get four. Maybe he could take an extra pill and get six, but the longer he stayed in one place, the better chance someone would notice him. This whole trip was *supposed* to be about not being noticed, but based on tonight's goddamned shit message, he'd already blown it. Somebody had been watching, waiting. Somebody who wanted him so bad they weren't willing to call the cops. If whoever it was tried to take him alone, or even with a handful of guys, Lafitte would kill them all right quick.

Still, he wasn't the same man he was in prison. He was weaker. He was in pain. He could barely keep his eyes open. So the Walmart Supercenter, open twenty-four hours and bright as shit, was perfect. There were already a few semis scattered there. His truck wouldn't stand out. He pulled in after sitting through a couple of cycles of the red-yellow-green, pretty sure he fell asleep during the first green but with no one behind him to honk. The florescent brightness helped him stay awake so he could circle until he found a spot two spaces away from an employee's truck and nose to nose with some college student's bland Corolla.

He turned off the engine and sat still for a moment, searching for leftover pain from the last wave. It was getting better. He didn't know when it would come back. He never did anymore. It was coming more often, every couple of days on its own, or sooner when he forced it—loading and unloading the truck, lifting weights, jacking off. He smiled. He could only guess what caused it, didn't have time to find out.. It had been months since he'd been online. He hadn't bothered to read any newspapers, either.

A few more deep breaths, a look around to see if anyone was paying him any attention, but would he really be able to tell? He'd stopped checking his tail barely ten minutes after leaving the truck stop in Hattiesburg, and he knew damned well someone had him on radar there. The pain, the sleep deprivation, the anxiety, shit, don't expect the man to concentrate much.

He hopped out and the humidity nearly dropped him. But there was a breeze, too, and the smell of salt water on the air was what really got to him. How many years had it been? Maybe he would drive on down to the beach in the morning to get a glimpse of the Gulf again. It wasn't the fastest way, but there were some things that needed to be done. He knew he might not get a chance to see it again after this.

Lafitte walked around to the back of the truck, slid the door up, hopped inside and dropped the door again. The lock clicked. No one would be getting inside unless they had badass bolt cutters or a welding iron. It was safe. There weren't too many places Lafitte felt safe anymore, so his truck had given him plenty of good sleeps, regardless of the heat, the dark, and the smell of diesel. The heat hadn't mattered when he was driving around the Midwest in the cold, but once the temps rose, he had rigged a car battery to run a handful of little fans. He slept on a puffy sleeping bag he'd scored through a garage sale. Not as nice as the prison mattress, but he slept much more soundly on it. The mound of fake boxes at his head hid a couple of pistols, his pain pills, his juice, and some cash. They also hid the trash can lid covering the hole he'd cut out on the bottom of the truck. From the bottom, any snoopers would see a rein-forced square of plywood. It was barely attached, easy to kick off. His escape plan. He hadn't had to use it so far.

He turned on his flashlight and crawled across the floor to his makeshift bed. Flicked on the fans, cooled the sweat soaking into his clothes. He eased onto his side across the sour-smelling sleeping bag and bunched up one corner as a pillow as the pain started to throb in his jaw and arm again. So he reached into the nearest box, grabbed a bottle of painkillers and half a bottle of warm water, and swallowed five of them. Then he drank the rest of the water, knowing he needed it, but goddamn if the warm stuff didn't turn his stomach.

Tomorrow. One more day of driving and it would all

be over by sundown. He yawned, tried to ease the pain by breathing through his nose, all the while praying for some peace. At the very least, right? Jesus, you can hate the fuck out of me if you want, but if I ask for peace, you still have to give me a little, right? Wasn't that part of the deal?

No answer. It was okay. There was never an answer. He just talked to the Lord to make himself feel better these days. They understood each other—no one had come to help Jesus off the cross either. Wasn't a damned thing to it.

# CHAPTER THREE

When Melissa woke up, she almost thought it was still part of a dream. She was on her stomach, cheek on a fluffy pillow, Egyptian cotton sheets on her skin. The chill of the A/C and the warmth of the bed and the slight but pleasant headache, the memories of the night before, made her grin and lift her feet until the sheets slid down her calves. She smelled coffee, but not the burnt heaviness of diner joe. It was clean and earthy. The TV was off, the shower running.

It was coming back to her. Melissa turned toward the windows, a long row of them, showing her only a deep cloudless morning sky. Her hair was halfway down her back, and she liked the way it felt, not all bound up for work. The alarm clock on the bedside table said it was close to noon. The push button phone beside it reminded her this wasn't DeVaughn's actual bedroom. This was a hotel suite. And from the look of everything, a really nice one.

It took her another few seconds to realize she had been sleeping in the wet spot.

It made her giggle.

She sat up and let the sheet fall and walked over to the windows, arms stretched wide, yawning, not at all ashamed of her naked body. Not like anyone could see her this high up, the windows facing the beach, but even if they could, she wouldn't have minded. She might have even enjoyed the attention. Maybe eight guys out of ten would look at her and cringe—the fat rolls, the cellulite, the sweat rash here and there—but those last two guys, they'd been all over her. And she knew she was good enough to get another two of those eight assholes to give it up.

Sexy was a state of mind. She'd learned a long time ago, watching how the black guys loved the curvy chicks, watching how the white guys would call her a pig, or a fucking whale, or make moped jokes, and she would sigh, shrug and tell them "Your loss." And sure enough, a couple of them would find her later, in private, looking around nervously, wanting...*something*.

Melissa was no slut, though. She didn't give it up for every high school boy who had given her corner-of-the-eye glances because she dared to wear short dresses, flip-flops, and heavy lipstick, a bit of the old '50s pin-up style that worked so well on larger women. No, *she* shamed *them*. Shamed them for having mocked her. Shamed them for thinking she was a vending machine. Shamed for not owning up to what it was making their cocks hard. Once they had apologized and groveled a little, she'd let them kiss her. She might rub her palm across the bulge in their jeans. It never took long. They didn't make fun of her anymore, even if they didn't stop their friends from doing it.

The one she lost her virginity to, he was the one who was not ashamed. Tall, truly and deeply black, with a French accent because he'd moved there from Haiti. All her rubbing did for him was make him grow larger, and larger, and she started to get worried. But what he did to her that afternoon, the second floor of the high school library while the final bell rang...yes, what she'd hoped it would be, not the disappointing stories of the skinny bitches with their jock boyfriends and the fumbling with the condom and the "I didn't feel anything." Fuck that. Melissa felt it. She felt it good.

Since then, a couple of lackluster semesters at Southern Miss between jobs at Waffle House and Lane Bryant and Walmart and then the truck stop. She'd figured out she wasn't college material. She'd told her mom, and Mom had shrugged and said, "Only thing college gets you is a job you can't turn off at quitting time."

She'd dropped out of school, she'd partied some—booze, dope, but nothing harder. She took too much pride in her fat ass to turn into a meth zombie. And yeah, she'd hooked up with a couple of other black guys before, a few wiggers, and a couple of country boys, the current boyfriend one of those, stuck somewhere between kid and "great white hunter" or some shit. Constantly in a trucker cap with the word "ass" on it somewhere. Or worshipping those Duck guys with the beards. Playing video games. Spending too much money on a pick-up truck he never hauled anything in, especially not the deer he kept claiming he had *almost* bagged. Always almost. She should have known better. He was one of the ashamed ones. But Melissa was getting older, almost twenty-six, and she hadn't found anything near enough to the way Phillipe had made her feel in high school.

That's why she took a chance hitting on DeVaughn Rose. He had been sweet to her last night at the diner. He looked older, maybe close to forty, but he had it

together. Money, manners, and class. The tequila he'd
been pouring into his coffee was top-shelf. She had liked
how long his legs were. Liked how he sat easy in the
chair, knees wide, slumping just so, and his voice was
just right, too. Rough but smooth, right? Deep but not
Barry White.

Whatever. She'd made a play, expecting to be shot
down because here she was in her diner clothes, stinking
of grease and sweat, hair twisted up, and not a trace of
make-up. Not even lipstick. Not even base. Zits on her
chin, not to mention where else on her body. But even
then, as she'd known since eighth grade, sexy was a state
of mind. Instead of turning her down, he had handed her
a twelve-dollar tip and asked, "You still want to give me
that ride?"

While standing at the hotel windows, goosebumps
rising on her arms and legs, her nipples growing hard in
the chill, Melissa let her hand fall to the hair between her
legs, fluffed it out. Crusty from his cum. At some point
she had decided DeVaughn wouldn't need a condom
with her. She was on the pill, yeah, but still made the
cowboy use ribbed Trojans. Same as every other man
since Phillipe. She'd gotten lucky with him, no baby, but
it had been a moment of weakness. If she ever felt
anything even close again, maybe she'd let the weakness
wash over her, but not sooner.

As soon as DeVaughn wrapped his arms around her,
the decision was made.

After calling her boyfriend and telling her she wasn't
coming right home—"What you doing then?" "Going
out." "Like fuck you are." "Well, I am."—she had
driven DeVaughn's Cadillac down to Gulfport, half-hour

to the south. He'd kept drinking straight from the tequila bottle, and offered her some. It was bright, sweet stuff. He wasn't like any man she'd been with. He could *talk*, really converse. He asked lots of questions about her, listened to the answers. He'd been around and could talk to her about Harry Potter and New Orleans history and eighties music, Prince and LL Cool J. But he wasn't into rap. His CD changer was full of blues and R&B, and he tried his best to teach her about it. This was the only bad part. Blues was boring. It wasn't Melissa's jam.

DeVaughn was all like, "You ain't heard Black Joe Lewis before?" and "Robert Cray, Smokin' Gun, baby. Listen to that," and "This here's Gary Clark, Jr., listen, listen."

Yawn. But, okay. Seriously, after a while the grooves actually made her feel relaxed, and the tequila kept her warm. She didn't mind he was wearing a tracksuit worth, what, several hundred bucks while she was in her diner-stained t-shirt and black pants. He made her not mind. Once they got down to the Coast, he told her to head toward Biloxi, then told her to pull up right to the front door of the Beau Rivage Casino. Let the valets handle the car. And they did, knew his name and everything. He held out his arm for Melissa and held his chin high and said, "Want to play some slots?"

The slots were fun, but not cause they won, cause they didn't. He wasn't worried about money. Fed in a couple of hundreds to last a while, then they kept on talking. She was telling him about the music that moved her, veering wildly between pop, hip-hop, and country, and about how she usually glammed up like a fifties rockabilly girl and how she really wanted to be a nurse or an x-ray tech because it was where all the money was. He laughed, said, "Girl, they just telling you that. Being happy is what makes you money, makes you *want* to go to work. Working for a paycheck, shit, there's enough of that in the world already."

"Are you telling me I shouldn't work? Let a man take care of me?"

He squinted at her sideways. "Shit, I'm not Beaver Cleaver. What I mean is you find what you want, and you show the people who do it that you're as good at it as they are. Even if you're not yet, you make them think you are."

She had no idea who Beaver Cleaver was. "How's that?"

He shrugged. "Before I became the man I am now, I was a mess, don't you know? I was a dumbass banger, but then I saw Phil Ivey on TV playing cards. Boy all Tiger Woods-looking, except knowing math and statistics and shit. I looked around my place, pretending I was some sort of gangsta. Shit, my brother had already got himself killed by a cop. I wasn't up for it no more."

"What, you play cards now?"

"Sure do."

"Like, blackjack?"

"Texas Hold 'Em. Poker, baby."

"And you're actually good at it?"

Big smile. Good teeth, no grill, no gold. "You just drove how good I am. You just gambled how good I am. And, baby, you want to, we can go upstairs and I'll show you how good I am."

They had a few more drinks—Melissa loved daiquiris—and wasted away another hundred before she took him up on it, and they were all over each other in the elevator. But this wasn't TV romance, no "fall into the room ripping each other's clothes off" nonsense. He led her in, offered her some bottled water, showed her the view, and then sat on the edge of the bed. Told her, as he took off his own shirt, "Let's take a good look at you."

Here she was the next morning, standing naked in a hotel suite overlooking the blue-green Gulf, miles and miles, thinking about how much she liked it last night. She came, what, three, four times. Wore her out. Then when he came, it made her eyes go wide and made her bite her lip and made her forget about Phillipe.

Her fingers slipped a little lower, across her pussy, still wet. Getting wetter.

Confidence. It had always worked before. Seemed to be working now.

She heard her cell phone buzz. Looked around, found her pants on the armchair, and pulled her phone from her pocket. Seven missed calls, six from the boyfriend and one from Mom. She listened to that one: "Tell your son of a bitch to stop calling me. He's pretty sure you're cheating on him. You've got to lie better."

Sigh. She texted the boyfriend. *Don't call me no more. Get out of my apartment by five p.m. If you're there at five oh one, I wouldn't want to be you.*

Dropped the phone back onto her pants, ignored the next buzz and walked across the room to the bathroom door.

There was DeVaughn, toothbrush in his mouth, shower running, steaming up everything, neck bent to hold his phone. "Uh huh. Uh huh. Uh...well, I don't know. I'll be there. Keep watching. Don't do anything. Sure as fuck don't fuck with him." He saw her reflection in the mirror. He smiled. A good sign. She mouthed "Good morning."

DeVaughn said, "I gotta let you go." He hung up the phone.

Yeah, definitely working now.

DeVaughn looked into the mirror and saw her standing there, stark naked with bedhead, and he thought, *Damn those eyes.* Something about them, he couldn't look away. The way she looked at a man, like, *I want you,* and there wasn't nothing the man could do but give in. And he was glad he did, because, *damn.*

Maybe because he was in a good mood. He'd finally done it. Finally seen Billy Lafitte with his own two eyes after all these years. So much had changed since then— this wasn't the same Coast Katrina had hit, not by a long shot—but Lafitte's name was never far from the front of his mind. If there was one person in life DeVaughn was sure enough going to kill, there he was. Last night, watching the man eat, watching him talk to Melissa like a normal person, watching him walk to the men's room to see the message on the wall, it had put DeVaughn in a righteous mood.

And this waitress, she'd been giving him the eye. Pretty eyes. Hazel. She was one of those women that had a small head and a wide body. A man might look once or twice, and maybe if that man was drunk or lonely, sure. She wasn't *ugly*, not one ounce. Just, you know, the situation. Greasy, stanky, some pimples on there, pimples on her ass, but, goddamn, she was *nice*. She could speak without speaking, you know?

So yeah, he took a chance while he was in a good mood, and the next morning he was still feeling good. Good God, man, the girl could *fuck*. Drained him dry. By the time they were done, both were sweating like they'd run a race, and they were laughing cause it was some funny shit. She draped her arm and leg across him, and he didn't mind it at all.

He got up, made some coffee, and watched her sleep. Girl had a husky snore on her, but that was okay, too. Something about her, he couldn't put his finger on it. No need to kick her out right away. They could go get some breakfast. Treat her to Waffle House. Maybe even go buy her a couple dresses from the Lane Bryant, see what she was like dolled up. It wasn't as if Lafitte was going to slip the net now.

His phone rang—a Little Richard yelp—and he fumbled it, went to the bathroom. No need to wake her. So he answered it in there, quiet.

Lo-Wider said, "We getting tired, man. He still ain't up."

"Y'all didn't take shifts?"

"Shifts? You didn't say nothing about shifts. We powered through on Pimp Juice."

"Shit nasty."

"It's not so bad, you add the Three Olives whipped-cream, man."

"And you wonder why you're tired."

"I'm only *sayin*. You coming or not? Or we got to bring him to you?"

"It ain't like that. We still need to follow him. I know

where he's going, I just don't know *when.*"

"Then you need to tell Crocker or Shack to take over."

"Alright, alright, I'll holler at them." DeVaughn reached into the glassed-in shower, separate from the bath, and turned on the heat, wide-open, with a little cold. The steam billowed out, fogged the mirror. "But don't let Motherfucker leave your sight. You stay your ass awake until they get there."

"Easy for you to say."

"Now you talking shit."

DeVaughn thought he heard something behind him. He looked in the fogged mirror, saw Melissa standing there, arm raised, braced on the doorframe. Hip cocked. The smell of her spread all over the bathroom, and those eyes were bright and wide.

"Rider, I gotta let you go."

"You *better* get Shack down here before I start snoring."

DeVaughn ended the call and set the phone on the vanity. "Morning, baby."

"Nice room."

"Yeah, they comp me here."

"I thought you might need some company." Eyes flicked toward the shower.

He could already feel himself getting thick. Damn, what sort of potion had she slipped into his coffee last night? No, he knew what it was. It was *confidence.* Some women made up for what they lacked in the beauty department with pure gumption. But this one, she was one hundred percent *damn damn damn.* He nodded his chin toward the shower. She teethed her bottom lip and stepped over, opened the door and slid inside. She held her head back in the stream and moaned nice and easy.

DeVaughn wrapped his hand around his dick. Yeah, Lafitte wasn't going nowhere today. And if he could help it, neither was Melissa.

# CHAPTER FOUR

*Lila Barbara Watkins named him.*

They called Lo-Wider "Lo-Wider" because he had a
Fat Albert belly going on, like he ate an inner tube and it
got stuck real low. Kid was nineteen and weighed three-
forty. Couldn't find his neck for all the chins. But, shit,
Lo-Wider sounded badass, much better than Fat Albert.

Right then, not even noon and the sun was turning
the car into a broiler. He was riding low in the passenger
side of his grampa's white Nineteen Ninety-Six Monte
Carlo SS, sweating a river onto the leather seats. He'd let
Bossman Steve take over the driver side because the
wheel had started to bruise Lo's stomach. Bossman Steve
was the white guy they let hang around when they
needed help. Only seventeen, on the football team,
defense, so that was how he knew Isaiah, the guy nearly
passed out in the back. This wasn't no gang-thing,
though. Mr. Rose had gotten out of the game when his
brother was killed and the cops who did it got away
with it. They were nothing but kids back then anyway,
but DeVaughn Rose, he was, like, famous to them. Man
had made some money with cards, and didn't even have
to cheat. The man still knew all the bangers, and
everyone in the Black Gulf Mob knew the man was
paying hella good cash for a real Lafitte sighting, and
Lo-Wider was friends with bangers, even though he
hadn't joined. He knew better than to even ask. He
wasn't no Biggie Smalls. He was just Big. So Lo-Wider

had gotten lucky up in Memphis, and had himself a taste of what DeVaughn was paying. He wanted more.

But god*damn* if this part wasn't bullshit, babysitting a parked truck all night. They'd burned up so much gas yesterday they couldn't afford to run the a/c anymore. What Lo-Wider had thought was, hey, this bitch finds a place to park for the night, DeVaughn comes in and pops his ass. Instead, it's more hurry up and wait.

"Bossman," Lo said. The white boy hated being called Bossman, but he'd finally started taking it without a fight. "You know Shack or Crocker's numbers?"

"Don't you got them in your phone?"

Lo-Wider held up his flip-phone. "Man, this pre-paid piece of shit?"

Steve shrugged. "Left my phone at home." But there was an outline of it in his shorts pocket, one of them Samsungs, big as a notebook. Steve was embarrassed he wasn't on those niggas' speed-dial. Not even on their slow-dial.

Lo-Wider shook his head. It had been about forty-five minutes since DeVaughn had told them to expect back-up. Still, wasn't nothing moving on the Muscle Max truck, at least not what they could see. Instead, they had to sit still and shield their eyes from the harsh reflection of the sun off the truck. Only Isaiah had sunglasses. Lo-Wider picked his shirt off his chest with thumb and index finger, gave it some flaps. It was as wet as if he'd been swimming.

"Shit, fuck this." He opened the door and climbed out. About the same heat as in the car, but the slightest breeze made it feel like Alaska. "It's *hot*."

Without his weight on board, the car bounced up.

Isaiah snorted himself awake and grabbed both headrests in front of him. "What's up? He moving?"

"Naw." Steve shook his head. "Lo getting bored."

"Fuck, I hear that. This wasn't what I expected."

"Supposed to watch him."

Isaiah leaned forward between the seats. "Yeah, but, you know, supposed to be exciting. Supposed to be something happen."

"Don't matter. We've got someone coming to relieve us. You want to get some Popeye's after this?"

Isaiah crunked up his face and eyes. "Shit, I didn't spend all night out here to miss out on the fun. I say we go wake this motherfucker up, scare the shit out of him."

"Hey." Lo-Wider hunched down, leaned through the open window. "We supposed to watch. Only watch."

"Man, I ain't going to touch him."

"Still, I'm just saying."

Isaiah scooted over to the passenger side and got out. Yawned and stretched. Boy was *tall*, man. But the problem with bringing Isaiah along as muscle was that's all he was. He didn't understand "Maybe." He didn't get "Just in case." It was fine dealing with high school punks or Vietnamese gangstas, but this guy, this Lafitte, motherfucker was a wanted man. He was straight-up dangerous.

Lo-Wider was losing control of this thing. "Man, come on, we did what we had to do. We bout to get paid, son."

Bossman Steve was out of the car, too, walking around to meet them. "We're not going to beat down on him. We going to kill some time, goof on him some. Call

DeVaughn and tell him this guy woke up, tried to leave. All we're doing is holding him down until someone gets here, then we can get some Popeye's. I'm *hungry*, man."

Lo-Wider flipped his phone open and hit redial and tried hard to hear over the traffic on Highway 49, semi-trucks, horns, low-end booms from decked out Nissans and Mitsubishis. The line on DeVaughn's went straight to voicemail. He hung up and dialed again. Voicemail. *Shit!*

He left a message—"Man, he's up, man, but we ain't got Shack or Crocker, man, what we gonna do? Call me. My boys are getting restless. Call me, man."

He looked up. Isaiah and Steve were already ten yards ahead of him. He closed his phone and tried to jog but he was no jogger. Hurt his knees, bouncing and shit. He wasn't going to catch up. He tried DeVaughn one more time. Still nothing. Told the voicemail, "What are we supposed to do now? My boys want to stop him, man. You'd better get down here."

Look at them: Isaiah wearing shiny black kicks, long black jeans shorts, black boxers blousing out, black jersey—fucking Bulls jersey, and he don't even *like* the Bulls. Bossman Steve even worse, in those fucking plastic sandals, the ones with the big Velcro strap across them, and *white socks*, for fuck's sake. Fuck. He was also in shorts too big for him, kept having to pull them up. T-shirt had skulls and swirls and shit on it. But Lo-Wider, what did he care about posing? Hard enough to find jeans that fit, a nice pullover Chaps polo. Old-school Adidas, size twelve.

Why they got to act like they got no sense? Why they got to act like they on TV all the time?

Lo-Wider was still ten feet away when Isaiah started banging on the back of the truck. Lo flinched, stayed off to the side. Afraid of bullets coming out the door.

"Man, it's wakey-wake time, you hear me? Open this motherfucker up!" Isaiah still banging. Bossman Steve following up with an extra bang or two of his own.

"That's right, nigga!"

Isaiah shoved Steve. "Man, what I told you?"

"You know I don't mean anything."

"And this dude's *white*!"

Lo-Wider did a whisper/shout sort of thing. "I'm telling you, shut up! You don't know what this guy can do."

Isaiah smiled. The sort of smile a kid had when he ain't had his ass kicked yet. No daddy or grampa around to put him in his place like Lo and Steve had had, although whatever sense Steve might have once had done got knocked out by his daddy years ago.

Isaiah kept his eyes on Lo as he slammed his palm against the back of the truck a few more times. "Come on out, motherfucker! Rise and shine!"

Lo-Wider willed his phone to ring. Anything, anyone.

They heard some rambling around from inside the back of the truck. Saw it bounce a bit on its springs. Finally heard the lock click. Then the door, slowly, slowly, slid up halfway, and there was this Lafitte motherfucker on his hands and knees, sweat-drenched uniform, looking weak as Steve's dad after another all-nighter of booze and beating on his current stepmother. Sleepy-eyed and more confused than mad.

"Is there a problem?"

It was the first time Lo-Wider had heard Lafitte's

voice. Low and flat. Full of gunk, full of pain. And now Lo got a better look at the man up close, he didn't know what to think. Lafitte was small, but under the skin those muscles were taut like the wire holding bridges up. Word was in prison, motherfucker was stacked, though. A tire pumped too tight. Up close, Lafitte wasn't as strong-looking as Isaiah. Someone had deflated him.

Isaiah steamrolled on. "Ain't no one tell you you can't park here without asking me first? I don't remember you asking."

Lafitte sighed and grunted, got his legs under him, sat on the edge of the truck. "I didn't see a sign."

"I bet you also didn't see a sign saying Free Parking, Stay as Long as You Like. Because it ain't here either. But there are rules, man. Rules."

Steve laughed. "Yeah, man. Rules to this sort of thing. And penalties, too. Like ten yards and loss of possession."

Isaiah screwed up his face at Steve. Steve stopped talking.

Lafitte didn't say anything for a long moment. He wiped sweat off his face with both hands, rubbed his palms on his shorts. Left a trail of mud, or damn near it. Lo couldn't tell you there was a grin on the man's lips, but it sure as hell wasn't no frown. Lafitte closed his eyes, took in a deep breath, and let it out slow.

"You hearing us? Don't we get an apology?"

Lafitte opened his eyes again. "Who're you with?"

Lo-Wider should've been the one to talk. This wasn't a gang thing. He was about to say it, too. About to say what DeVaughn had told him to say, in case something like this happened. Was going to tell him "an old friend" had sent them. "An old friend who wanted to say hello." Those were the words, right on the tip of Lo's tongue.

Isaiah beat him to it, saying, "Who said we're with anybody? The fuck does it matter to you?"

"Sure as fuck not Royals, I can see that. Disciples? Maybe you're Disciples."

Isaiah puffed out his chest. Lo-Wider said "Hold up—" but didn't get anywhere because Isaiah finished with, "We Mob, motherfucker. Mobsters all the way."

Steve tossed his hands in the air like he just didn't care. "BGM for life, baby!"

There it was in Lafitte's eyes. The recognition, as DeVaughn had promised. Lo's stomach churned.

Lafitte shook his head, and now he really was grinning. "Mob? Shit, and here I was thinking I was in real trouble."

"Watch it now, motherfucker."

"I don't want to offend you guys or anything. Seriously, though, how is the Mob still around?"

Isaiah and Steve, cheerleaders that they were, couldn't think of much to say past, "Shut your hole, faggot."

And "Piece of shit homo."

And "You open your mouth when I got something for you to put in it. Right now you listen to me."

Lafitte turned his face to Lo-Wider. Raised his eyebrows, like, *You with these idiots?* Then back to Isaiah. "Listen, I'm sorry. I'm sorry I parked in your parking lot in front of your thrift store and next to your Waffle House. But I'm moving on soon. What do you need, money? You want some money? You want, oh, I don't know..." He looked over his shoulder. "Vitamins? Protein shakes?"

"I said to shut your hole."

"I can, hold on." He held up his hands wide, then did a dainty thing with his thumb and middle finger, locking his lips.

Bossman Steve was on edge, barely able to stand still. "No he didn't. Dis. Re. Spect."

Isaiah's muscles quaked beneath his skin. He was drum tight. Lo-Wider stepped back. Stared at his phone. Still nothing. Jesus, man, where the fuck was DeVaughn?

Isaiah took a couple steps closer to Lafitte. "I didn't ask for money. I didn't ask you to suck my dick. All I asked for is some respect, but the cracker in you can't even do that to save your own ass. Can't even respect a nigga for ten seconds to keep from getting whupped. So now I'll tell you what I want. What I *require*. It's going to be your blood. A whole bunch of your blood. And I'm going to take it the hard way."

The last bit got lost because before Isaiah could say it, Lafitte was on his feet again inside the truck and bringing the door down hard. Isaiah, God bless his soul, made a grab for the fucker's leg and missed and the latch on the door landed right on his wrists and *holy shit fuck motherfucker* was there some screaming, and Isaiah recoiling his hands as the door popped up a foot. Lafitte slammed it all the way closed this time.

Lo-Wider squinted like he did for horror movies, but he got a good peek at Isaiah, now on his ass on the asphalt, holding a purpled wrist. Broken glass in a water balloon. Seething through his teeth and saying *Shiiiiiiit-ahhhhhh-shhhhhiiiiiiiiit.*

Steve banged on the truck.

*Coward this! Faggot that! Motherfucker!*

*Motherfucker! Mother—shit! Cheap shot piece of shit! Fuck you up!*

*Gonna fuck you up! You can't stay in there forever!*

Lo-Wider's gnarled-up stomach was going to go full diarrhea soon if this didn't calm down. He glanced around the lot. Mommies coming out of the stores were staring. People pumping gas were staring. People at the counter in Waffle House, turned around, staring. One of them fuckers was going to call the police. Sure as shit they were.

Steve still banging.

*Piece of motherfucking ass!*

Isaiah still seething. Writhing. On his back now, full roll going on.

Steve still banging.

*Going to FUCK YOU UP! You hear me? BGM for life, motherfucker! BGM—*

Steve went down hard on his back. Took Lo-Wider a second to figure out what was going on. Lafitte had grabbed the kid's ankles from underneath the truck.

How the fuck—

Lo-Wider could've sworn—

Steve kicked and scuttled his way out from under the truck. Lafitte rolled out and hopped up before Steve could flip himself over. Lafitte grabbed him at the waist, a fistful of oversize shorts, and lifted him like a sack of potatoes.

"Who sent you? Who's been watching me?"

"*I don't know, I don't know, I don't know.*"

"But you BGM for life, ain't you? You following orders, ain't you? Who sent you?"

37

"*I don't know, please, please, I wasn't going to do nothing, please.*"

Lafitte dropped Steve, who let out a whoosh of air and a yelp. Lafitte stepped over to Isaiah and knelt beside him. Isaiah was out of his mind with pain. Rocking back and forth. Cradling his hand. Lafitte reached in, grabbed him by the crushed wrist. The scream that came out of Isaiah was enough to make a man piss his pants.

"Who sent you? Tell me. I know who it was. I want to hear you say it."

"Is, is, is." Deep, rattling breath. "Is, is, is...oh God, fuck, Jesusjesusjesus."

Lafitte squeezed a little tighter. "Say the fucking name already!"

Steve had gotten up and launched himself for Lafitte's back. Wrapped a forearm around his neck and got him in a sleeper. Lo-Wider knew better. Sleepers never fucking worked. Wrestling was fake. It was all fake. Learned when he was thirteen.

Lafitte, red-faced, stood. Steve had a few inches on him, bent him backwards. Steve tightened more and more, cutting off Lafitte's pipes. Lafitte hooked his fingers on top of Steve's forearm, but he couldn't pry loose.

Steve's eyes, left right left right, looking for help. Isaiah near tears, fetal position. Lo-Wider, no way. Not worth it. He stood where he stood and shook his phone. *Ring, motherfucker, ring.*

Lafitte planted his feet and opened his mouth wide and let out a scream and *wrenched* himself forward, lifting Steve off the ground, over Lafitte's head. Lafitte reached back, took the kid's leg, and sent him over, hard, headfirst onto the pavement. Lo-Wider heard the loudest eggshell crack he'd ever heard, and Steve went limp on his back except for herky-jerky in his legs, arms. There was a lot of blood.

"Shit, no, shit, no." Lafitte swallowed air and crawled over to Steve. Slapped his face. "Shit, no, shit, wake up kid. Shit, wake up." Held a palm in front of Steve's face. "Shit!" Leaned his ear to his chest, listened. "SHIT! SHIT!"

Started two-handed pumping Steve's chest. "No no no no. Goddamn it. Not now."

Lo-Wider watched. Wasn't getting it.

Lafitte shouted over his shoulder. "You! Fat kid! Got a phone?"

Lo-Wider too stunned to answer.

"You fat fuck, do you have a fucking phone? Get an ambulance. Get a fucking ambulance now. Right the fuck now!"

Lo-Wider looked at the phone in his hand. He'd forgotten how to use it. It was telling him he had a missed call. Shit. DeVaughn, finally. But too fucking late. He dialed 911 and was all "Something bad happened. Real bad. Just...hurry up."

They wanted to keep him on the phone. Wanted details. Wanted his name. Wanted *something* more than "Send a fucking ambulance." But that was all Lo-Wider had for them. Said, "I need 911. I got two of my friends. One dead. One might be dead." For real to him now.

Lafitte was still pumping Steve's chest. Still chanting "Shit." And then, ear to the chest again, he went slack. He gave up. Whispered "shit shit shit."

He pushed himself onto one knee. Waited. Hard breaths.

Even Isaiah had calmed down enough to say, "Why you stop? What you doing? What? Keep doing it, man. Keep doing what you was doing. Come on, man."

Lafitte ignored him, grimaced, held his left arm tight against his body like maybe Steve had hurt him some after all. Sirens on the air, closer and closer. And they weren't just the EMT sirens. Lo-Wider could tell. Lafitte could tell, too. Isaiah turned his sights to Bossman Steve and was all, "Hey, wake up, white boy. C'mon, now, we having fun is all. Steve. Steve. Steve. Wake up, now. I said wake up. Listen to me, boy, I said to wake up!"

Lafitte turned and walked over to Lo-Wider, who was about to piss his pants, and he started crying immediately and said, "I swear I didn't. I never told them to."

Lafitte shook his head. "It's DeVaughn, right? DeVaughn Rose still around, isn't he?"

The shitty cell phone in Lo-Wider's hand rang and buzzed again. Two times. Three. Lafitte plucked it out of Lo-Wider's grip. Easy. Looked at the name and number displayed. Then back up at Lo-Wider.

"Listen, we was only supposed to watch. We weren't supposed to mess with you none. I swear."

Lafitte slipped the phone into his back pocket. The sirens were louder. The number of looky-loos had grown. Many of them had their own phones up filming this. Lafitte turned to his truck, then started looking around at the other cars in the lot. Lo-Wider knew what he was thinking. Didn't take him even half a minute to finally hold out his hand, palm up, and he didn't even have to speak. Lo-Wider fished his key from his pocket and handed it over. "It's the Monte Carlo over there, behind the gas station."

Lafitte took the key and said, "Thanks," and jogged toward the car. Lo-Wider watched him go. What was that shit, saying "Thanks"? Like Lo-Wider was really helping because he wanted to. Like he had a choice. Motherfucker was breathless, too. If it had been a fair fight, Lafitte would've been done, man

The motherfucker hopped into Lo-Wider's grampa's Monte Carlo and revved it up. He was gone in seconds, blending in with the traffic on 49, heading up to I-10, as the first cops were hauling ass into the parking lot. It killed Lo-Wider to do it, what was necessary. His two friends, pretty good friends, one dead, one real bad off, suffering. He hated to do it. The cops came to a stop. There was an ambulance coming, too, right behind them.

One of the cops stomped over to Lo-Wider while the others swarmed the two on the ground, some stupid racist motherfuckers with their pistols out, aimed toward Isaiah. Not a one bothering to aim at Steve. They swarmed the Muscle Max truck, too.

The cop, a lady cop, with a thick braid, was in Lo-Wider's face saying, "You, did you see what happened? Did you call this in?"

Lo-Wider shook his head. "I don't even have a phone. I was using the bathroom in Waffle House."

After telling her a few more times, she moved on to find a better witness. Lo-Wider started for the gas station. He was going to need a ride and a new phone.

Finding new friends would be a lot harder. Lo-Wider sniffed and tried not to look back.

He mumbled, "BGM for life, motherfucker."

# CHAPTER FIVE

The thing was, DeVaughn didn't even know somebody was calling. Didn't know his phone had shut down. Too busy with Melissa in the shower, which turned into exactly what he thought it would. Then after, her putting her stank-ass diner clothes back on, and DeVaughn shaking his head, saying, "No, girl, this won't do."

After cutting the call from Lo-Wider when Melissa stepped into the bathroom, he had held the button down too long, shut the whole thing off. Then they spent so long in the shower that by the time they got out, they were in a hurry to get moving. He picked up the phone, glanced at it. No light for a missed call or an email, so he shoved it into the front pocket of his gray chalk-striped slacks and escorted Melissa down to the front and waited for the valet to get his Caddy.

"So first we get you dressed fine, like you deserve. Then I'll take you out for some real good food. You like seafood? You're from here, you ought to."

Melissa liked it a lot. Fried catfish. Hush puppies. Boiled shrimp. She slapped her rump. "I like it so much, I'm surprised this right here ain't turned into scales yet."

They laughed. They were laughing all morning, laughing at nothing, touching each other constantly. It wasn't anyone else's business. So they hit the mall and first had to get her some pretty panties, pretty bras.

DeVaughn was surprised to see how much sexy could fit into a size twenty-eight, but it was a good surprise. He sat in the chair outside the waiting room while she tried them on. And finally she said, "I can't come out there in this."

"Then how am I going to see?"

"You come in here."

He looked over at the salesgirl nearby, not bad herself, who grinned with her heavy red lips and fifties glasses and didn't say a word. DeVaughn went into the changing stall, a tight fit with Melissa's girth and his long legs, and he watched her try on a whole bunch of different panties and bras and they were all nice—the thongs were best, but the boyshorts, they cupped her just right. And she had cleaned up real nice, too. Even though she'd used the same soap and same shampoo as he had and no perfume fog, girl smelled *clean.* When he was getting so hard it hurt he finally said, "Shit, buy them all" and tried to hide his erection as he followed her out to the counter. He paid in cash from his roll. It was a fun way to pay, made people wonder.

Outside the store, he pulled his phone from his pocket again. Still no lights, no missed calls. He was about to give Lo a wake-up call, lazy-ass teenagers, when Melissa told him JC Penney's had great dresses for fat girls, and she grabbed his hand, walking fast ahead of him, an excited kid heading for the toy store.

This was nice. This wasn't his usual day, but it was nice. Lots of his mornings were either just getting to bed after all night games, or getting up late, or Xbox, or a run along Beach Boulevard to keep himself in as good a shape as possible, considering his recent lifestyle adjustments. Those young bangers, they didn't have to do a goddamned thing to stay toned. Now that DeVaughn was creeping ever closer to forty, he felt it. Shit, not even his daddy lived to be thirty-four. Complications from diabetes, they told him. Not going to happen to DeVaughn, uhn uh. No way.

Another thing was, walking around the mall holding hands with a white girl in Mississippi? Not so big a deal anymore. Bunch of middle-school girls were doing it all around him. Lots of the high-school girls in shorts showing off their business, draped over black guys like they *wanted* you to know it. Maybe their daddies didn't know about it, but you could bet your ass their mommas did.

Of course DeVaughn had had himself some white women before, but this girl, today, man, she made him feel different. They'd hooked up *one night*. Only one. He was getting pissed at himself for acting a fool. *Had* to be cause of Lafitte. Had to have made the difference.

Melissa sure enough was right about Penney's. She picked out some sharp-looking retro dresses, bright and tight. Splashes of green and white, some orange, some Indian-type designs. All of them mid-thigh, showing off her curves. DeVaughn's favorite was black with a rectangle of deep red making up most of the front. He shook his head like *Damn!* when she modeled it outside the dressing room. She twirled, lifted her knee, shrugged one shoulder. The dressing room was next door to the kids' clothes, and some of the white mothers shopping with strollers or noisy toddlers on leashes were giving them the evil eye. But that made Melissa show off even more.

While she ducked in to change into the next one, DeVaughn checked his phone one more time. Still no lights. Shit, what were these guys thinking? He had to call Lo-Wider now. It was damn near two in the afternoon already. He slid his thumb across the screen. Got no response. Did it again. Fucking phone.

He pressed the power button. Waited. Instead of the photo of him holding up his prize money from his third place win in Pensacola, he got the "wake up" screen.

Panicked. "Motherfucker."

A bit too loud, because a white mother shushed him and pointed to her kids who were giggling and weaving in and out of the racks. Probably already knew all these words, the way they acted.

Things could be so fast now, these phones, these pads, these computers, but didn't it feel like a goddamned eternity waiting for this motherfucker to come back on. DeVaughn paced around the aisle. Shit shit shit.

Staring at the phone. Willing it to work. And there was his own smiling face and the nine-thousand, seven-hundred and forty-five dollars he'd picked up after twenty hours and getting his trip sixes beat by a full house. And then all the little app icons. And then the damned thing buzzed and lit up and there were eight missed messages, all from Lo-Wider.

He listened to the messages—pleas at first, then frantic cursing, then hardly anything. The last one was road noise and nothing else.

All he'd wanted the boys to do was watch Lafitte and follow him if he went somewhere. Okay, so DeVaughn hadn't called Shack or Crocker for back-up, too distracted by Melissa's big ass in the shower, but still, all they had to do was *watch*. This wasn't about no attack. He had plenty of time for that. He had to find out where Lafitte's woman was first. He couldn't tell the boys, couldn't tell these baby-bangers doing his errands for pay, but this was some very personal and intense shit. Wherever Lafitte's woman was, DeVaughn needed to be. Lafitte had to be heading at some point. The man don't show up on his home turf with the whole fucking nation manhunting him unless he's going to see his crazy ex-wife. That just don't happen.

And all this time, he'd been at the mall, shopping like a bitch. Shopping *for* a bitch. What would the Mobsters say about it?

A couple of other missed calls, but not a number he knew. No messages with them. He did a quick reverse search, saw it was a gas station next to the parking lot where Lafitte had parked. DeVaughn guessed it was Lo-Wider, finally getting tired of no one answering the cell phone.

He dialed Lo-Wider's number. Rang four times, went to voicemail. He hung up, called back. Four more, and voicemail again. *Shit, that is stone-cold disrespect right there.* Another hang-up, another dial-back. This time, he answered on the second ring. More car noise. Barely a grunt for hello.

"I'm sorry, Lo, I'm sorry, listen, my phone, it shut down. Listen, tell me where you are, I'll be there. I'm on my way to the car, I promise."

No answer.

"You can't be mad at me, son. I've got business to do. Lots on my mind. If y'all had done what I'd asked."

Then Lo cleared his throat and said—wait, this wasn't

Lo-Wider. "DeVaughn, I'm still here."

Hadn't heard the redneck cracker's voice in years. He'd never forgotten it, but shit, live in his ear once again.

"Jesus, Billy."

"I'm still here. Next time, how about you and me? Leave your niggers out of it." Hitting the—*er* hard.

And that was that. The call was cut.

"You okay?" Melissa's voice behind him.

He turned. Worried lines around her mouth, eyes. The dress, purple with dots, not so good. He dug into his pocket. "Something came up. You want those, I'll leave you some money. I've got to go."

"What? What came up? What do you mean?" As if he hadn't said a thing about money or dresses. As if he'd broken her heart.

"I can't say. It's real personal."

Melissa's lips got tight and she looked away, toward the tween section. "Oh, I get it. Seriously. Fuck it, I'll go home. I don't want the clothes. I don't want the money. Fuck."

Bitch be getting mad. Made DeVaughn pause. Made him think. "No, it ain't like that. It ain't like that at all."

"It's always like that." The tight lips gave up and she let out a sigh. "It's okay. It's fine. It was a nice night. It was really nice."

She was thinking about calling the boyfriend again, thinking about the fight she was going to have. Thinking about the sort of cocksucking she was going to endure to make things right after the same ol' same ol'. And here she'd thought...yeah, DeVaughn read every word of it in how she blinked her eyes, a little misty.

"Listen, I mean it, listen." He touched her chin, got some eye contact going. "You and me, okay? We good. I want you to buy those dresses, all of them except this ugly ass polka dot shit. You too fine for polka dots. You go back to the room, play some slots, whatever you want. I *promise*, baby. I promise."

Held her eyes, held a fingertip under her chin. Jesus, and here he thought he'd learned better. Don't be falling for no pussy. Especially white pussy. You fall, you break your neck. But, goddamn, they all say that but then they all end up falling at some point too. He said her name. "Melissa. Please."

She finally wiggled her nose and her lips, pouty. Still blinking. "You know, fuck this."

He had hoped she wouldn't say it. Like a steak knife in the throat. He cleared his. "Alright, listen—"

"No, wait, I'm not done. I'm saying fuck this macho, got to deal with it on your own, hiding your business from me bullshit. If you're really telling me the truth and this is different? Then I'm coming with you."

He shook his head. "You don't want to get into all this now. Come on. Next time."

She laughed. Nervous, angry laugh. The steak knife had slipped from his neck to his balls. "No, uhn-uh, no. You want to be with me, you really want to be with me—"

He was already nodding.

"Good. Then *be* with me. Literally. LIT-ER-RA-LY." Licked her tongue on those last few. Let him get a lingering view of it."

He swallowed. "Damn, baby."

"What was it you told me about reading people? Play

the man, not the cards?" Melissa stepped closer, her toes touching his alligator skins. "I don't care if this lasts one more day, or a week, or until Christmas, or the next ten years. The deal for today is simple. Don't treat me like a slut, alright, and I won't treat you like a playa and we stick together this one day. *One day.*"

She could have taken the words right out of his mouth. It was some sort of magic and shit. As soon as his phone call had ended, he had felt sick to his stomach all the sudden. She must've felt the same, because she nailed it. They needed to be together today for some reason. No matter the code, no matter the reason. He grinned.

"Girl, leave all the diner shit in there and change into the red one."

Melissa looked good when she smiled. Made up for the harsh parts of her. "I'm going to need some shoes."

# CHAPTER SIX

Soon as Lafitte closed the phone, he winced and held his breath a good long beat. Then, shit, thought about DeVaughn. All this time, and that piece of shit was still hounding him. Lafitte had never forgotten when he and Paul shot down DeVaughn's brother, sure enough. Remembered every moment. The little bitch had betrayed Lafitte and Asimov to their own kind—cops. Probably would have sold out DeVaughn, too, if they hadn't shot him. Guess it didn't matter to DeVaughn. Blood was still thicker.

The shit message on the truck stop wall—DeVaughn. Son of a whore had found him somehow, something the whole FBI couldn't do.

Not as bad as he thought. DeVaughn was just one guy, maybe with some baby bangers doing his dirty work. But DeVaughn himself still banging? Sad, man. Sad.

Another wince. The pain was subsiding. His head cleared and he thought *I've got to get this car off the road.* Fast, fast, fast.

Up ahead, a rest area. A nice big one, too, teeming with semis. Teeming with SUVs. He pulled in and parked far down the line, where people took their dogs to shit. He had forgotten that Mississippi rest areas were little antebellum oases, with white columns and honeysuckle, surrounded by a pine forest.

He stepped out and closed the door. No need to wipe it down. Cameras everywhere these days, the parking lot full of them. It was hard to get lost anymore, and sometimes the best way was to stand outside, stretch, yawn. Hide in plain sight. At first. So he did. His shirt was soaked. His shorts were clinging, chafing. He needed full lungs of magnolia-scented air. Two. Three. Then he scoped his choices.

A little car. There was a Fiesta, a Focus, a Corolla, a Kia, another Kia, a Honda hatchback. He couldn't trust the newer ones—GPS gadgets and satellites and computers able to track his ass all over creation.

A pick-up truck? The only one here had flames on it. Back-window stickers, Calvin peeing on a Chevy sign, something else he didn't recognize, probably about hunting. Educated guess. Big tires, too. No, not worth the trouble.

None of those SUVs, either. Just…no.

Which left the old man standing next to two touring motorcycles.

Wide, clunky, built for old people who weren't RV types. They had always wanted motorcycles, but couldn't afford them until they retired. By then, they had lost sight of what made them love motorcycles anyway, except for the part about seeing the country. So they bought "touring" bikes and hit the road and met up with thousands of other retirees with touring bikes, and they wore leather jackets and chaps and communicated via hand signs that made them feel like part of the club, even though it was bullshit. It was the retired people's club, if it was anything. Steel God had laughed it off once—"It's mutual masturbation, two fingers at a time."

These bikes, Jesus. One was tan and red and had deep red saddle bags, while the other, the one the man was right next to, was a little sleeker, black and silver, but it was just another touring bike with sharp corners. All flash, no substance.

It was Lafitte's best way out of here, too.

The bikes were a good fifty yards away. Lafitte did a quick search for the other bike's owner, found her as she opened the door to the main building.

Let's get this over with.

Lafitte walked over to the old guy with a smile on his face, shaking his head. "Now that's some mighty fine road machine right there."

The old man, startled at the voice, straightened up and laughed and said, "Thank you kindly. It's a great way to see the country."

"Are you a lifer? Been riding all your life?"

"Oh, no, no. A whim, really. I bought these a couple of years before I retired. A good five years ago. All they did was sit in the garage." He shook his head. "Until one day, I couldn't stand them getting dusty anymore. Now we've put four thousand miles on them the last six months."

The old man was wrinkled enough to be, what, seventy? He was thin but strong enough to handle the bike. He wore brand-new jeans and a long-sleeved T-shirt, Indian motorcycles logo, tucked into his waistband. Lafitte could take him, but it would be tough in a stupid way. He couldn't overestimate.

Then the old man started pointing out specs. "Thirty-five miles to the gallon. Eighteen-hundred cee-cee, six cylinder—"

"Yeah, listen, I don't care."

The old man gave him a shit-eating grin. "Excuse me?"

"I'm going to steal your bikes now. And you're coming with me."

The wife was on her way back. She was probably the same age as the man, but looked Vietnamese with jet black hair under a New Orleans Pelicans cap. Lafitte grinned and waved at her. She waved back.

Lafitte said, "You're going to be nice and quiet and we're all going to leave together on your bikes, okay?"

The old man was already backing away, turning to his wife. "Hey, Tish—"

"No, wait." Lafitte stepped closer, reached out to the man. "Don't be stupid. I can take you with me right now, us two only, and I can break your neck and toss you in the ditch, or you can let me ride your wife's bike with her riding with me, and I won't kill either one of you, I promise."

The old man's cheeks grew red. The wife was still oblivious, walking up to her husband saying, "What is wrong? Are you okay? What is wrong?"

Lafitte gently placed his hands on each of her shoulders and steered her from her husband's side before he could fuck this up any more than he already had. "We're going for a little ride, is all. I'd like to see how you bike feels."

"Okay." She looked over her shoulder. "But I ride with my husband?"

"No, you can ride with me."

"No, I ride with my husband." She tried to twist from his grasp, but Lafitte held on and guided her to the bike.

54

"No, it's okay, really. You ride with me." He reached over for her helmet, handed it to her, and he climbed onto the bike. Damn, this felt good. Now he was a wall keeping her apart from the old man, and she was not as fit as her husband.

The old man stalked around the bike and got his finger wagging in Lafitte's face. "Now you listen to me, you...you...troglodyte. How dare you. How dare you."

"Can we go, now? Hurry it up, please." He grabbed the wife's arm, and she let out a whine, but she grabbed hold of Lafitte and climbed on behind him. Lafitte said, "You're making a scene, mister, and I'm taking your wife no matter what, so, let's hit the road."

"I most certainly am not going to let you—"

Lafitte vroomed the bike and it felt like an old friend shaking his hand. From his balls to his fingertips, goddamn, it had been too long. The old man's face, beet red, his mouth, slack. Lafitte stabbed his finger at the man's bike a few times. "Get on, get on, get on."

The old man hustled, got to give him credit. Hustled into his helmet, hustled onto his bike. Tish held on tight, her bony hands poking him in the ribs. He looked back over at the security guard, who had his eye on them but hadn't bothered to get off his cozy little perch and see what was up. Dumbass.

Lafitte walked the bike out of the parking spot, throttling up some noise, still waiting for the old guy to get his shit in gear. When ready, Lafitte gunned the bike onto the interstate ahead of a semi. He looked back. The old man was gunning it even harder to keep up. Guy was going to fight to win. That was enough to earn Lafitte's respect. Of course it was a stupid thing to do. Old man should've run for the security guard as soon as Lafitte took off. Should've got the whole state descending on Lafitte's sorry ass before he couldn't even make the next exit. But love conquered all. Love made you stupid. Love. Fuck love.

Lafitte thought, *Good for you, old timer.*

They headed east in a hurry.

# CHAPTER SEVEN

Motherfucking embarrassment was what it was, DeVaughn having to go, hat in hand, to those motherfuckers in BGM to beg for help. He'd paid Lo-Wider and his boys cold hard cash, and they couldn't manage to keep it straight, so what were these baby gangbangers going to do when it was just a favor? How much was this really going to cost him?

He met up with the new third-in-charge of the Gulf Mob—couldn't even bother to send the number two—on a pier in Biloxi where these idiots had tied up rented jet skis. All wore baggy shorts, long white tees, a couple shirtless. The number three, who called himself One O Four because it was his junior high locker number or something, was covered in salt spray, arms crossed. Oakley sunglasses and a grill. Always behind the times, the Gulf Mob. Whatever was out of style, they stayed on that shit a good year or two longer. It took DeVaughn getting out of the gang himself to finally see it.

DeVaughn never really "got out." Nothing official or shit. One day, he simply wasn't there. He went away on a trip, stayed longer than expected, and by the time he got back, Black Gulf Mob had moved on. Fine with DeVaughn. Took a load off his mind.

So here he was in a suit, Melissa in a new dress showing off the goods, while the fools loping around on the pier acted like someone was filming this shit.

"My nigga!" Open arms. One O Four was shorted than DeVaughn. The motherfucker wanted a hug. What was up with hugging? Now DeVaughn's shirt was damp, his coat was damp, and he smelled like cocoa butter and weed and beach stink. Melissa stood back. She had a Jackie Kennedy thing going on, her hands together in front, pleasant grin on her lips—bright red.

One of those bangers was playing hip-hop on his phone. The others were tossing in a phrase here and there. One O Four looked past DeVaughn at Melissa, put his thumb to his chin like he was inspecting a painting. "So what's going on here? Are we talking or are you bringing us a gift?"

DeVaughn laughed. "Melissa's a friend of mine. She goes where I go."

"Shit, man, you're supposed to keep this shit private in your barn, not drag her out in the light of day."

Another banger said, "I'm blind, I'm blind!" As if looking at the girl had done it.

DeVaughn turned his head. Not a word from Melissa. She didn't give up the grin. Stood still. He mouthed *Sorry*, but she blinked at him, like, *Not your fault.*

"I mean," One O Four said, "that ass, I feel you, but, damn, son."

DeVaughn nodded. "I don't have a lot of time."

"I feel you, I feel you. Just playing. So tell me what's going on."

"Asking for help, man. I had hoped I could talk to Bark about it—"

"Bark's busy. Bark's really busy."

Bark was the one in charge these days. Been a lot of different ones in charge since DeVaughn was part of it.

Wasn't no cult of personality. Loyal to the colors but not to the man.

Bark was just another one.

DeVaughn lowered his voice. Hadn't said this sort of thing in a long time. "*Glocks,* man. And some soldiers, man. I ain't got a lot of time."

One O Four: "Whatever you need. Long as you can pay for it."

This shit. "Lafitte's back in town, man."

"Luh who?"

Goddamn, they were young. "Lafitte? One of the cops who killed my brother, man. Lafitte?"

One O Four nodded. "Okay, okay, I feel you, I feel you."

"So...my brother was BGM."

Nodding like a bobblehead. "Right, right."

Jesus, where was that motherfucker Bark at? "I need some extra eyes on him, man. I can't keep up on my own."

Big smile. "Thought you already had it covered, what I heard."

"What's that now?"

One O Four said, "Something about you giving up some green for those eyes already, I heard, when you could've come talk to us first. You done fucked up, so what makes you think BGM will work for free?"

DeVaughn set his jaw. Smelling his own sweat out here now was no fucking picnic. Quick look at Melissa, still standing like a good, respectable lady, Mona Lisa lips, looking off into the water.

"Look, we're all in this together. This is about family."

"This is about cash money, nigga. This is about me and these boys with me that will do whatever you want as long as we see your bank roll first. What you got for me?"

"I'm asking for help here."

"Son, you ain't asking for shit. You paying. You the one turned your back on the Mob to go play cards. This ain't family. Your family is long gone. BGM's got a reputation to protect. So I need to see cash up front, enough to keep all of us happy while we watch for this white boy you talking about."

DeVaughn thought about the cash in his pocket. He'd already spent more than he could afford if he wanted to play in the New Orleans tournament. Getting Lafitte was more important, but he still had to make a living. "I got a thousand."

One O Four laughed. "And I got a whole lot of other shit to do."

"Fifteen."

"Hundred? Listen, let's be real here." Thumb on his chin again. "I know what you rocking. I know about your card game in New Orleans, and I know you got to have at least ten K on you. I'm not greedy, but I also ain't stupid. You need some change left over to impress your lady here. Shouldn't take much. Drive her through a Wendy's and you all set. Listen. Five of us here, we'll give you the family discount. Fifteen *each*. That'll leave you enough for some slots, a Motel Six, and three helpings of Long John Silver's for your whale."

Whoa, boy, that got them laughing.

Even more when Melissa stepped around DeVaughn and slapped the living fuck out of One O Four.

DeVaughn couldn't tell if One O Four was playing or not, staggering until he nearly fell off the pier before one of his back-up grabbed hold, pushed him in front of the girl again. DeVaughn was ready to take him out if he struck back. But Melissa towered over the wannabe godfather. One O Four was all wiry muscle, tight tight *tight*.

She went, "You disrespect me all you want. I love French fries, I love pizza, I love Mickey D's, too, and it shows. You'd still ride it if you got the chance, but you're not ever going to get the chance."

"Shit, bitch—"

"Did I say talk, boy?"

*Ooo, white bitch call him boy.* Got himself a chorus.

"What I am telling you, are you listening?" Hands on her hips, leaning in. "You don't disrespect your elders. Especially one who can buy and sell your sorry slave ass."

Before he could react, she lifted her foot without looking at it, pulled off her flip flop, and started slamming it against his ear. This time there wasn't no play-acting. It really did motherfucking hurt, and he really did try to shield himself as he dropped onto the pier and curled into a ball. She took her bare foot and pressed it hard against his cheek and said, "You going to tell Bark to call DeVaughn. You going to tell him he's lucky DeVaughn *asked* for help instead of just taking who he needed. And you ain't getting one goddamned dollar."

She gave her foot a twist and stepped back. She threw her flop down, flipped it right side up, and she walked past DeVaughn to the car. A diva. Shit, wasn't nothing else to say. DeVaughn turned to follow her.

One O Four was still seething and saying, "Shit shit shit" but got it together and said, "Got some fat bitch doing his talking for him? Like I got to respect that?"

DeVaughn looked at him and said, "Yeah, I think it would be a good idea."

He followed Melissa to the Caddy. Should be mad. Like One O Four said, he didn't need no fat bitch doing his bidding. Wasn't what no man did. But he was grinning. He was watching her sashay. He would watch her do anything. He'd watch her take a dump and like it. He'd never felt this way before.

When he caught up, he said, "You could've got yourself beat."

She tossed her hair. "Him? I've been hit harder by bigger men."

"Baby, Goddamn! You can't be all up in my business, understand?"

She stopped in front of the Caddy and turned to him. Her stomach pressed against his as she smoothed his suit coat and fixed his shirt collar. "Something a man should know. The less he has to say, the stronger he is. There ain't one of those assholes thinking bad about you right now. They thinking bad about One O Four, though. Let's go get something to eat and wait for Bark to call you."

"Yes ma'am."

But before they stopped to eat, he pulled in behind a liquor store, put the car in park. He turned up the radio a little, commercials right now.

He gave her a look. She looked back, a little pissy. "What?"

He gave her a chin. "Girl..."
Melissa got it then, teethed her bottom lip. "What?"
"Lay your seat back."
Grin. "Oh yeah? Again?"
"You better do it."

She let her seat drop all the way, set her right foot on the dash, hiked her left leg up so DeVaughn could crawl over on top of her, then she braced her left foot against the steering wheel. He was already unbuckling. She took over while he helped push her dress up past her hips.

They fucked nice and hard and quick, didn't even get to the next song on the radio. He lay there on top of her, her fingers grazing the back of his neck.

He was breathing hard, but asked her, "Damn, what is it 'bout you?"

She said, "You already know. No need to put it into words."

Good enough for DeVaughn. When he was soft again, he slipped out of her pussy and said, "So, Long John Silver's?"

She shook her head. "You and me, we need to be *seen*. Someplace nice, with waiters and shit."

So that's what they did.

# CHAPTER EIGHT

The patient's mother always stayed later than she should've. The nurses had stopped warning her because whenever they did, they got a cold stare in response, enough to put them off asking again, let alone wanting to mess with that type of Jesus she worshipped, the old-style Pentecost. Everyone else at the facility was convinced, even though the woman proclaimed she loved Jesus and her screwed-up daughter, she sure as hell didn't love much else.

Mrs. Hoeck took her time, and the staff waited her out. It took Ginny a while to settle down after visits from her mother. They'd explained to her mother over and over, "She's very anxious after your visits."

But her mother always said the same thing. "I'll pray with her. That should make everything all right."

It never did. Made it much worse. Made her daughter believe wishes might come true. And so Ginny would wander the room, waiting up all night for the man who would never come. No use telling her mother, though. It was almost as if she wanted Ginny to stay this way instead of helping her get better. Maybe it was why Mrs. Hoeck kept reminding Ginny about her suicide attempts, about Ginny's own daughter, Savannah, asking about Mommy, and the news about "that man," the one she would never call by name, as if keeping him alive in Ginny's restless mind was supposed to be healthy. The nurses thought she did it to keep her hooks in.

When the doctor finally confronted Mrs. Hoeck about it, she said, "He's a demon. The moment she forgets he's there, torturing her spirit, is the moment he wins."

Jesus Christ indeed. But as long as the insurance kept paying to keep her, the doctors and nurses would do their best to undo the damage while Ginny's mother would come rip their stitches out the next afternoon.

But the one thing Mrs. Hoeck had never told Ginny, the one thing she had *forbidden* the staff to tell her about under threat of lawsuit and pulling her daughter from the facility, was that her son, Hamilton Lafitte, had died. A ten-year-old boy, killed in a prison riot in North Dakota. As far as Mrs. Hoeck was concerned, regardless of how much it held back her progress, that information would never, ever be given to Ginny.

The funny thing was, Ginny had forgotten she had a boy at all.

So another visit, another three hours of nearly wordless Ginny, listening to her mother ramble on, judgmental, sarcastic, indignant, as she kept Ginny up to date on the family, the church, and the awful state of America thanks to "President" Obama. It's not that Ginny wouldn't talk. She would, sometimes. She answered questions during the day. Simple things—what she wanted to eat, what she wanted to watch on TV, what music she wanted to listen to—but not much else. Never on her own initiative. Only yeses and nos, nods and shakes. But to Mrs. Hoeck, it was as if she was carrying on a full conversation with Ginny, never stopping for a response. The woman must have *imagined* her daughter was talking to her, making more than a few nurses wonder if they were taking care of the wrong family member.

After all, Mrs. Hoeck was the one who had watched her grandson die in a cold, soulless prison. She was the one who had been nearly raped by an inmate. She was the one who had been forced to escape through a hole in the wall and climb a fence topped with razor wire during a blizzard. She was the one who cradled Ham's broken head in her lap as they raced to the hospital, far too late.

Who could blame her for having a screw loose? Who could blame her for embracing the Old Testament's God of vengeance rather than the Jesus she wouldn't shut up about?

Who could blame her for passing along her hate and despair to her only daughter now that Lafitte had been responsible for the death of her son, her grandson, and her daughter's sanity? Ginny's father had shut himself down, married to his wife in name only. The only reason he stuck around was because he was too old to divorce her, and because he wanted to help raise Savannah, somehow shield her from her grandmother's influence.

After another marathon visit, the nurse waiting at the station reading Rachael Ray's magazine until the frigid Jesus-bitch passed by, not even a "thank you" or a "good night," the nurse counted to ten and then walked down to Ginny's room. She found her as expected, in her cozy chair, wrapped tight in her satin robe, wide-eyed and rocking.

"Saw your mom today?"

Ginny nodded. Didn't look at the nurse.

"Did you have a nice visit?"

"Yeah."

The nurse gathered the wrapping paper from the floor. Always wrapping paper, always gifts. Slippers and magazines, gospel CDs, Christian novels, ones Ginny never read. They had told Mrs. Hoeck to stop bringing so much stuff. But she kept on, and the nurse kept collecting it all, adding it to the box in the closet.

"Are you tired? Need a nap?"

Nothing. The nurse had her back to Ginny, though. She looked back over her shoulder. "I said, are you tired?"

Eyes closed tight. Ginny shook her head. She had petulant little-girl face.

*Great, another long night.* "That's okay, hon. That's okay. Whenever you're ready." The nurse was forty-two, a single mother of a twenty-year-old son with two DUIs already, a maxed-out credit card with another one getting fuller by the month, and she hadn't had any sex she could remember in two years—and only one time she couldn't remember, but it must not have been any good, from the look of him the next morning.

So fine, another night of pretending to be Ginny Lafitte's best pal, all the while hoping she would fall asleep, because having to talk to her like she was a helpless child was the top indignity in a job full of indignities. Even more so than cleaning up piss, poop, puke, and jizz. At least those sorts of duties were expected. But something about Ginny...always on the verge of attempting to end her life unless everyone tiptoed, and even that didn't always help. It was exhausting. The nurse wanted to ask her, "If I hand you the knife, will you do it right this time?" And Ginny would surely nod, eager. But she'd never get it right. She didn't really want to. She wanted to throw a tantrum and make a mess.

What a bitch.

Instead, the nurse sat on the stool opposite Ginny and asked, "Any music today? Your mom brought a new CD."

Ginny shook her head, a little grin. Her way of saying, *I hate the CDs Mother brings.*

Not even a thank you. Day after day. The nurse let out a sigh and said, "Okay. I'll drop by later. You know how to buzz me."

Back to the station. Back to the rotation. She had a handful of other patients to check on before she could get back to her magazine. There was nothing in it she cared about, but it gave her something to do to keep her out of trouble. There was a patient, a nice man, maybe close to fifty, still with all his hair, thick, dyed-brown. He flirted with her, even though he was in for some sort of alcoholic psychosis episode. Nothing would ever happen. She didn't want it to happen, and was ninety-seven percent positive she could will her way out of it happening, but she could still fantasize about it. She could still...

The nurse continued her rounds after Ginny's room. Around the corner. She passed a delivery man. She was off in her own world, not even thinking about him, but she shook herself out of it and turned. "Excuse me?"

He stopped.

"It's just me right now. I'll take it."

He nodded. Grinned. Walked back over and handed her the envelope.

"Do I need to sign for it?"

"No. It's fine."

"Thank you." Big big smile. A mouthbreather. She checked the label. The envelope was for another department. Idiot. She looked up, but he was already gone.

Fuck it. She'd wait until Loretta was on shift to take it down herself. If she'd given it back to this one, the damned thing might've ended up in Mexico. She tucked it under her arm and headed off to get her nightly dose of compliments and innuendo.


People tended to overlook delivery men. It didn't matter if the uniform said UPS or Muscle Max. Didn't matter how secure the unit was supposed to be. Lafitte was a delivery man with a padded envelope. Another thing about delivery men. Everyone assumed someone else had already cleared them. Otherwise, why would they be in the building at all?

Especially a sweaty, stinking man covered in road dust. Of course someone had let him in. Ah, the working class. The doctor in the elevator with Lafitte, a resident in scrubs, glanced over from his phone for only a couple of seconds, probably looking forward to the day when he felt less like the delivery man and more like his bosses.

It was probably a good thing Lafitte had passed off the envelope to the nurse already. She wouldn't expect to see him again. He had waited until he saw his ex-mother-in-law leave the building. He had figured out Ginny's almost-daily routine weeks ago—a few phone calls, a few lies. That was all it took. People wanted to tell you things they shouldn't. People *loved* to. They really did. They believed any story you told them. And in case someone did, hang up on them, then call back later when someone else was working.

The letters helped, too. Those fucking letters she sent him.

In fact, it was very likely the nurse he had passed the envelope along to was the one who had told him about Ginny's day-to-day life, mostly so she could have someone to vent about Mrs. Hoeck to. The nurse's name was probably Tabitha. Or Loretta. One of those.

Billy Lafitte had laughed and told her, whichever one it was, "I know. I've met her, too."

Ginny hadn't haunted his dreams in a long time. He hadn't seen a picture of her in, fuck, six, seven years? He hoped she was as mute as they said so she wouldn't scream. Would she even recognize him?

This was the door, open barely a smidge. Only the dimmest light coming from behind it. He looked left, right, and stepped inside, starting his mental stopwatch. Someone would notice. He didn't have long. The room was lit only by a nightlight, and the shades kept out most of the sun. Lafitte searched quickly, found the camera, and did his damnedest to keep out of its sight. He pulled out the bottle of spray paint he'd picked up at a store along the interstate, hopped up in front of the plastic square high on the wall, and sprayed once. Another hop, sprayed twice. Enough to block out the camera.

Only then did he dare turn around.

Ginny was sitting in her chair, a slightly pouting sort of look. Her frizzy dark hair was much shorter, peppered with too much gray. Her face was lined and pale and tired. She was sad, sunken, and, in his eyes, beautiful. "Billy Lafitte, you're very, very late."

"Sorry."

"I've been waiting, you know."

He started toward her, some of her letters crumpled in his hand. He fell to his knees and buried his head in her lap, shaking violently to hold back tears. She took off his cap and stroked his hair.

"I've been waiting a long time."

# CHAPTER NINE

The tiny bar was in a tiny restaurant in Beaver Bay, Minnesota. It was a two-story prefab building, a vinyl-sided block with three shops. The restaurant had a small sign above the door announcing "Lemon Wolf Café", flanked with two carved wood sculptures—one bear, one wolf. Across the highway was Lake Superior, right behind a couple of "antique" (junk) shops and the town post office. He liked it here because it was quiet, only three chairs at the bar, no one bothering him, and instead of a bartender, one of the waitresses would stop and refill his shot glass with bourbon, hand him a new bottle of beer, one of those small-craft IPAs that tasted so bad it was hard to get drunk on them.

But Franklin Rome drank it anyway, each bottle tasting better than the last. He'd usually eat the restaurant's catch of the day—Lake Trout, most of the time—after downing eight, nine, shots, and five, six beers. He got quiet when he was drunk. Not melancholy. No, melancholy was every day. "Quiet" meant "barely functional".

Most of the time, he was the only black person around for at least a good square mile, he thought. Sometimes the only person of color, period, including Indians. He'd been up here on the North Shore since after the jailbreak, after Colleen had fucked up so bad at the prison. She had been good to her word, though, and left him out of it. Some agents had come to talk with him in Minneapolis, and he had lied his ass off about the price on Lafitte's head, Colleen's part in all this, and the eighteen grand up for bounty. As soon as he'd heard about the jailbreak, he got online and scattered the money all over, ten times over. Stock trades and PayPal and offshore internet gambling accounts and more. Shit, the original account wasn't even in his name. He'd found it going through his wife's papers, a small savings account in her maiden name she must've opened as a child or teenager, but which had been forgotten along the way. Happened all the time. Grandparents put a hundred bucks into it and then ten years later, everyone has moved on. Out of sight, out of mind.

So he scattered the money, lied to the Feds, and quietly retired—although he'd pretty much been out of service for three years already, acting as a "paid consultant". In the end, he had to leave Colleen twisting in the wind. He'd told her if it all went bad, he would do what he could for her. But in the end, it came down to nothing. He had no pull, no weight, and honestly, he didn't give enough of a shit about what happened to her to even try.

Eight years in prison. She had a chance at parole in a few. If she got it, Rome would be ready for her. Plenty of guns in his cabin. Maybe the HIV she'd caught from the gangsta would kill her first.

The white ladies who ran Lemon Wolf were polite enough to Rome. He'd been coming here for about four months. They had never gotten past small talk with him, though. In fact, he was pretty sure they didn't know his name. He wasn't sure he'd ever told them. It was a place to drink that wasn't his cabin. Some food that wasn't from a microwave. It wasn't the sports bar up the hill from his cabin, a bar full of "bros", white ones, and their bitches and a bunch of noise. Occasionally, retired white people staying at the lodge next door would wander into the sports bar, too, and listening to their conversations drove Rome up the wall—boring talk about boring things from boring people. None of them were ever rude to him, not directly, but no one ever tried to really talk to him.

He didn't blame them.

When the Lemon Wolf was ready to shut down for the evening, he stood from his seat at the bar and waited for the world to stop spinning. It took a couple minutes, always did. The ladies always told him "Good night." They never asked if they could call him a cab—if there even were cabs in Beaver Bay—or get him a ride, even though he was obviously extremely inebriated. Perhaps they wished he would glide gracefully off Highway 61 into the depths of Superior, never to be heard from again. Not one worry in the world about the money they would lose—he was drinking a bottle of their bourbon per week alongside countless craft beers at a steep mark-up, especially in the off-season—as long as the lonely black gentleman no longer haunted their small café night after night.

Once he felt up to walking, hands still braced on the short wood bar that looked as if it was made by one of the lady's husbands in a garage, he fought down a burp and, as usual, gave the place one last look. In between tables were wooden dividers, each hung with local art for sale. None of it was much good. Lots of owls and bears and shit. But he liked the colors. He liked that someone was *trying*, for fuck's sake.

Out the door, a little stumble here, there, until his hands were on the hood of his Jeep Grand Cherokee. A lease. He kept hoping to hit a deer with it, but he hadn't been so lucky yet. The next burp, he lost the fight. It came up loud and full of acid and he hated himself. This was his life now. His wife, Desiree, dead by Lafitte's gun. His attempt at revenge, all fucked to hell and back. He had now made a new enemy in Colleen, who had been his closest ally in hating Lafitte. Whatever power he had as an FBI agent had evaporated, all favors revoked. No friends left, almost. The few who remained, he'd pushed away. No one had his new cell phone number. No one knew where his cabin was. No one.

Or so he had thought, because as he somehow made it the couple miles back to his cabin, easing down the hill, ready to accelerate if a goddamned buck wanted to step up to the challenge, he found a car parked out front. A Chevy Malibu. Sitting on the trunk, an old friend. Wyatt had risen higher in the ranks of the State Police to Captain, but tonight he was just an older man in jeans and a plaid short-sleeved button-up. Rome didn't want to see him, since, you know, he couldn't think of Wyatt without thinking of what happened to Desiree in that hotel stairwell.

Rome parked beside the Chevy, got out, shook Wyatt's hand, hugged him. "You found me."

"You made it easy."

"I didn't mean to. Come on in."

They went inside the cabin, which was pretty ritzy by cabin-standards. Seriously, Rome had sold almost everything that was worth anything to make sure he had enough for this place—three hundred thousand and change—and a modest retirement account for booze and microwave dinners, newspapers and wi-fi, a lease on a Jeep Grand Cherokee he hoped might one day be the end of him.

Cozy, faux-wood cabin styling, one big living area, a bar separating it from the kitchenette, a loft for his bed, and a Jacuzzi tub in the far corner. Windows all around, a to-die-for view of the lake. The lake was Plan B if he never hit a buck. He hadn't quite decided between drowning out there sometime this coming fall, right before it turned to ice, or simply drifting off to eternal sleep after a handful of pills, a bottle of Four Roses, and a recording of Desiree's voice playing in the background, those voicemails he kept and listened to in the late hours almost every night.

Rome offered Wyatt a beer, but the trooper turned it down, said, "A bottle of water?"

"I don't do bottles of water. Tap?"

"That's okay."

Rome sighed, filled a glass with water, no ice, and brought it over. He led the way to the leather couch and armchair, flicked on the lamp, very soft light. He took the chair, and Wyatt eased onto the couch.

"Nice place."

"The last one I'll ever own."

"You're too young to think like this, you know. Hell, even I'm too young to think that way."

Rome grinned. "You know what I mean."

"That's what I'm worried about."

"You here for an intervention? You by yourself?"

Wyatt took a sip of water, looked around for a coaster. Since there weren't any, he held his glass on his knee. "I probably shouldn't have come. I mean—"

"But now you've come, so get on with it. I promise, I'll listen politely."

"You don't get it. I come bearing gifts."

"Of gab?"

Wyatt leaned forward, reached for his back pocket and pulled out a block of folded papers, tossed them on the end table on top of all the water rings from Rome's whiskey glasses. Son of a bitch could've set down his glass at any time if he'd been paying attention. Bugged the shit out of Rome. But he kept his tongue still and picked up the papers, unfolded them. They were printouts of digital photos, terrible quality. But they didn't need to be great to capture the images of a bathroom wall, three-foot tall letters smeared onto it, shouting WELCOME HOME LAFITTE.

"Well, fuck me. Is that shit?"

"Yessir. Written in shit. Yes indeed. This one was going around Instagram last night, and it got flagged by my Google search for Lafitte. Hattiesburg, Mississippi truck-stop. Some truckers took pics on their phones and posted them. But keep going."

A photo of Lafitte in a delivery truck. Sure as shit it was him.

Next one, Lafitte delivering boxes marked MUSCLE MAX to a strip-mall store.

Another. Another.

The alcohol in Rome's blood swirled down an imaginary drain. "What the goddamn—"

"That's him, ain't it?"

"That's him." Rome flipped back to the first one, the shit letter. "Someone thinks they've got a line on him, someone from his past, or they wouldn't be bothering."

Wyatt nodded. "I've heard some stories this past week, some sightings. This last one, the shit-writing, was a surprise."

Rome sat back in the chair. Tension, released. He took a deep breath.

Wyatt said, "You're dying to know."

"I am."

"No, they haven't got him yet."

Rome rubbed his hand across his mouth, his stubble, his chin. "But he's there. Holy shit, he's there. Motherfucker."

"So, should we call? Give the police a heads up?"

Rome cut his eyes at Wyatt. "Shit."

"I'm just saying, we're kind of far away, you know."

Rome looked at his watch. "When's the next flight to Mobile?"

"I thought you might want to know. Out of Minneapolis, six in the morning."

Rome rolled his head on the back of the chair. "I wish I could still fly whenever I wanted."

"So, what did you think of my intervention?"

"You're coming with me, right?"

A nod. "Told my wife I need about five days. Fishing trip. But the moment it starts to look dangerous, we call for back-up. Agreed?"

"Goddamn. I mean, *goddamn*." Rome started laughing. "Nobody ever said he was smart. Lucky, but never smart."

"Let's get moving. Two hours back to the Cities, some time to get you coffeed up, couple of tacos in you. Not sure what we'll do for sidearms yet, but I'll make some calls."

It sounded too good to be true. Convenient, too. Now? As Rome had settled on fading away? As soon as he had decided to let down the guard in his head? The one chanting, *Avoid drinking and driving. Avoid solo walks along the shore. Avoid hitting deer with your car.*

"Tell me something, then. This is you and me? Vigilante style? Nothing official?"

Wyatt cleared his throat. Scrunched his eyebrows. "You need this. Even if it's a goose chase, you need this. Could be we don't find him."

That was what the man was counting on, Rome could tell. A good ol' road trip, fueled by righteous anger. It could turn out to be absolute horseshit. Still, nothing better to do these days. Rome could die alone later.

He pushed himself out of the chair. "Let's go."

He reached for Wyatt's hand, latched on hard. He really meant it this time. "Good to see you."

# CHAPTER TEN

By the time anyone figured out something was wrong, Lafitte was gone and Ginny was dead.

The nurse, Tabitha, spent too much time in the drunk's room. Giggling, posing, responding to his filthy innuendoes with pretend shock. "My my my! Sir!" It wasn't until Loretta gave her a warning ding that she realized how much time she'd wasted. Even worse when she stepped out into the hall to find Loretta running toward her.

Out of breath. "When was the...the last...checked on Ginny?"

She pointed at the room behind her. "Right before—"

"Her camera. Her camera is out. Come on."

Tabitha, kicking herself, *literally*.

Then, "There was a delivery man. It was for the wrong floor."

Loretta's eyes went wide. "Hurry."

Lafitte took the stairs hard and fast. He was filled with, fuck, couldn't put words to it. Hate? Pity? Grief? Grief? Was it grief? How could he do what he'd done? Why didn't he try to talk her out of it? Because it wasn't

Ginny. It was a shell of Ginny. She would never be the same. It was all his fault.

But more to the point, she had asked him to. Those letters, week after week. No idea how she had found out where he was. No mention of their children. No mention of their past together. Just the request.

*Help me die, Billy.*

Out the doors. Keep up the walk, don't falter yet. He needed to get back to the bike. He'd abandoned the old couple, alive and well, in the woods north of D'Iberville, slashed their tires. He'd kept on driving. He'd got here and found Mrs. Hoeck's car, same one Ginny had told him about, and parked far enough away to watch for when she left. He had to keep going until he got to the bike. Tight chest, the pain in his arm and jaw ratcheting up. Breathing through his nose, mouth clamped shut.

He hoped she failed.

Did he really? Didn't he want her happy? Didn't he want what was best for her?

No, he hoped she failed. But he wasn't about to stick around and find out because he was too sure she'd get it right this time.


Tabitha and Loretta couldn't get her door open. Blocked. They pounded on it, "Ginny! Ginny! Is someone in there? Do you need help! Ginny, we're right here! Ginny!"

Some of the patients roamed into the hall, and some of them tried to help get the door open. The chair had been wedged against it, a devastating angle. Loretta called security. The guards tried to muscle it open.

"Jesus!" One of the guards. "Why can't they open outward?"

Tabitha got on the phone to the police. The facility went into lockdown.


Lafitte's head in her lap. Years since the last time. Her fingers brushing through his hair. Warm skin. A low hum in the air, a noise she made without thinking about it. They didn't need to talk, not much. They didn't need to catch up. They'd never had that problem. They *got* each other. Billy was terrible for her. Terrible, terrible, terrible. But still, in all that terribleness, there was some sort of connection, right?

They both knew there wasn't a lot of time.

"Sorry," he said. "I'm so sorry. I can never say it enough."

"It doesn't matter."

"Forgive me."

"Never." She kept stroking his hair. "That's not how this works."

He lifted his face. Clenched his jaw. Killing him. "It's my fault, I know, I know, but she shouldn't have brought him to see me. I told her to never bring him to see me but she did it anyway."

"Brought who?"

"Ham."

"Who?"

He blinked. "What?"

"Brought who? Who brought who? Who are you talking about?"

"Ham?"

"Who's Ham?"

"You don't know who Ham is? Hamilton? You know Ham. *Our* Ham."

Ginny bit her lip. Shook her head.

"Savannah?"

Shrugged.

He looked into her eyes and saw nothing there. Nothing. Not an act, not repression, not...anything. Nothing.

"You and me. We have a couple of, *had*, a couple of kids. A son and a daughter."

She said "Mm hm?" Still nothing.

"Would you change your mind about this? For your daughter?"

She placed her palm on his cheek, kissed his forehead. "Don't say anything else. I don't want to be here anymore. No one should have to live if they don't want to."

He pushed himself off the floor. Could barely stand to look at her.

She said, "You promised."

"How do you know? I never answered your letters."

"You're here."

Stupid question. "Jesus, Ginny." Throat gone dry.

She inched forward in the chair, her knees against his chest. "You promised."

"Not until you tell me you know who our kids are."

A twitch? A sigh? Anything? The pain crept down his left arm. He tried to breathe the pain away through his nose. He knew it would be a losing battle.

Nothing in her empty eyes, nothing on her empty face. Nothing. Nothing. He remembered both nights they had to go to the hospital. Or, one was night, the other was five in the morning. He remembered the times she told him she was pregnant. Remembered angry sleepless walks from his bed to the crib only to have the anger dissolve like sugar as he picked up his boy, picked up his girl, and they paced until they stopped crying.

How come she could just...forget? Or not even forget, but believe it never happened. How come he couldn't do that? He would love to forget what he had seen...he would give anything...

She whispered, "You promised."

He nodded. No time left. "I can't."

"You *promised.*"

He squeezed his eyes closed, squeezed her hands. "You and me. We can leave right now, you know. I can show you what you're missing."

Tight lips, petulant warble. "I don't need *you.* I need you to do what you promised. *You* are over. You are why I'm here. But you're also the only one who can do this."

"I've got enough guilt on my mind." Thinking, *What next? I take out Savannah, too?*

Ginny's breath grew faster, heavier. "You. Promised."

"I lied. I do that a lot. I won't help you, you know, finish up. I came all this way to tell you, Gin. As long as I'm alive, I need you to know that."

She wasn't listening. She pushed him back, unbuckled his belt, slid it through the loops of his shorts. He tried to hold her hands still before she could get it out. "Not now. We don't have time. Come with me."

She kept tugging the belt, her breath sharper, turning into grunts. Against his better judgement, Lafitte felt his throat go thick. His cock, swelling. This was what she wanted? Suppose there were worse ways to be apprehended than in the middle of fucking your ex-wife.

Lafitte let go of her hands and she slid the belt all the way out. But then she carefully curled it up, set it in her lap and stroked it like a kitty.

So that's what she had wanted.

"You promised." Stern.

He exhaled a shaky one and pushed up off his knees, looked down at her one more time. "Yeah," he said. "I guess I did."

He turned his back on her and slipped out the door.


Three shoulders to dislodge the chair. They fell into the room. The door, something behind it, bouncing back, hitting one of the men in the face. Tabitha was right behind him, determined to get in there. It was on her watch, it was her mistake to fix.

Her scream and the injured man's "Mother*fuck*!" hit simultaneously.

The coat hook behind the door.

Ginny, swinging from it, a belt around her neck. Already gone. The men pushed Tabitha out of the way, lifted Ginny off the ground. One unlooped the belt from the hook.

"Room! Give us room!"

Tabitha backed away until she hit the foot of the bed, stumbled but righted herself. She should be the one giving CPR. These guys—two security guards and one she didn't know who he was—jumped into action while Tabitha froze. Loretta was on the room's phone, shouting the emergency code again and again.

Tabitha didn't have much of a view, but when the men shifted she could see Ginny's face, pale, eyes too wide. Her neck, a deep cut from the belt. It couldn't have been more than a few minutes. She should be okay.

Chest compression, one, two, three, four, *Stayin' Alive, Stayin' Alive.*

Loretta raided the emergency bin, came out with a bag—a resuscitation mask—and threw it over. The third man placed it over Ginny's face and started pumping.

Tabitha felt helpless. At first she was thinking, then whispering, and then shouting, "What do I do? What do I do? What do I do?" And then, "What did I do?"


*What did I do?*

Lafitte was on his knees beside the motorcycle, his whole left side tensed, his arm tight against his chest, withering. An old man. A mummy.

He wished he could puke, but he didn't have anything in him. He didn't have time. He didn't have time for this bullshit pain, either. Fuck it, he should've looked for drugs—nitro, pain pills, fucking morphine—but he had beelined for Ginny. Fucking Ginny. Fucking...

Maybe if she'd shown the slightest bit of...what? Fucking. Just, what?

In those letters, she said she would keep trying to kill herself if she could, but they wouldn't let her. Her mother didn't want to talk about the "deeper" issues. They had tried, oh Lord, had they tried. But Mrs. Hoeck would shut down any such talk and threaten to take her daughter elsewhere, someplace more "spiritual", which, knowing about Mrs. Hoeck's brand of spirituality, was enough to make the therapists back off. It was a sick cycle to watch—mother wanted to keep daughter from killing herself, but had no self-awareness she was part of the problem. The ex-husband, obviously, but the mother made things much, much worse.

But Mrs. Hoeck knew better than all the doctors, all the therapists, all the theories, all the science, and one nurse had whispered, "More than Jesus himself, I bet."

Ginny wanted to die. Period. She had for a long, long time. Being forced to stay alive was the worst thing that could happen to her. Lafitte regretted it already. He had planned to come and take her with him. Pick her up and carry her outside to the bike, then run away and hide together. One day, when she was back to normal, they would come back for Savannah.

But in the room with her, the empty shell of a woman who didn't even remember they had children together, he let her take the belt. Fine. He hoped she would fail or someone would get to her before she could get it over with and it wouldn't be him who had broken the promise.

Fuck Ginny. Fuck Ginny. Jesus.

The alarms, sudden but faint. They had found her.

Fuck Ginny. Fuck Ginny. Fuck her. Fuck this. Fuck Ginny. Fuck Ginny.

The sirens—police, not ambulances. Faint but stronger by the second.

Fuck her fuck her fuck her fuck her—

Behind him, across the street, he heard someone shout, "Hey, you! You with the bike!"

Time to go.

\* \* \*

Emergency docs took the place of security guys. How long had it been? How many minutes? Tabitha heard ribs crack.

"Nothing?"

"Nothing. We've got to go, go, go!"

Pretty soon Ginny was gone, rolling down the hallway surrounded by damned good emergency medics, doing all they could for her, while Tabitha slid to the floor of Ginny's room. Was it worth it? The flirting with her psychotic drunk on a shift that depressed the fuck out of her? The fun of someone, *anyone,* wanting her sober?

The delivery man.

The administration had told the staff a long time ago to be on the lookout...

But, no, it had been years. No one really expected...

The ex-husband.

But, goddamn it...

She scuttled across the tile until she was back on her feet, running behind the lifesavers in the hallway. "The husband! He was here! He was here!"


Lafitte had gotten up to speed, zipping in and out of traffic, heading back to I-10, wanting to go west again. Really, no idea where to go, but the Mississippi Gulf Coast was a magnet for him. Gulfport, Biloxi, Ocean Springs, his old stomping grounds. He grew up here. Lost his Mom here, a drowning. Got arrested here as a teenager, shit, how many times? Loved cops. Goddamn, cops were cool. Became one himself.

Weaving through tree-lined side streets and parking lots, trying to remember the quickest way back. He came to a four-way stop a block off Mobile Street, which could get him onto 98, maybe. Just him and a Cadillac. Lafitte's turn to go.

Not even halfway through the intersection when the Caddy gunned it and slammed into him. Not fast enough to knock him too far, but it got the bike all tangled up under the bumper and front wheels. Lafitte's leg, bruised but not pinned in. Lucky. Goddamn.

He tugged his leg free, swung it over. The exhaust pipe had burned his other leg but he'd had worse. He was off and rolling away, Trying to feel all the places it hurt. Nothing but bruises, cuts. He was good to go. He sat up, turned back to the wreck.

A fat girl in a pretty dress got out of the Caddy's passenger side. Glossy lips. Familiar, maybe? And then DeVaughn Rose climbed out of the driver's seat with a pistol pointed at Lafitte.

Fuck.

The girl was almost giddy. "Kill that asshole. Get him, baby. Quick and easy."

"Motherfucker. What he did to my brother, seriously."

Pistol was shaking. Left hand.

"Dead is dead. Do him now. Get it done."

The gun bucked and went *blam* and Lafitte had been ready, ducked and rolled right, then on his feet before the second shot, behind him. He ran straight toward the girl's door and slammed into it with his shoulder. Made her fall back. Got her calf between the door and the frame. Her head bounced off the roof. Fucker wasn't going to fire the gun toward her, was he? She was letting it loose, too. Howling. Goddamn. Look around, Billy.

Edge of the suburbs. Brick facades on businesses, tax assessors and accountants and shit. More people pulling up to the four-way stop now. Was DeVaughn really going to shoot at him again, with people watching now? With his bitch singing in pain?

The aches caught up with Lafitte, his arm, chest, jaw. Ahead of him, a small parking lot in front of a lawyer's office. Four cars spread out. And the wide open world behind it.

Count to three.

One, two...

Take the fuck off and hope to fuck there's not a bullet gaining on you.

Flat out. Past one car, two, a glimpse of people staring at the scene from inside the building, through the blinds.

No shot.

DeVaughn shouted over his girl's screams: "Mother-*fucker!* I will find you, mother*fucker!*"

The farther Lafitte ran, the more DeVaughn's bullshit faded into fuzzy noise. *Run* even though your heart is aching. *Run* even though your heart is breaking.

Fine time to sing.


Tabitha gave her statement to the security guard, then the cop, and they all got hung up on her mistakes while she thought, *Are you going to get him or not?* Turned out she wasn't so good with details. She saw a guy in shorts and boots and a cap, carrying a package. Package guy. That was all. A little beardy. But as for eyes, hair color, scars, nose, lips, and whatever the fuck was written on the back of his shirt, Tabitha was useless.

She waited in the hall outside the Operating Room, pacing. Loretta had passed in and out several times now without speaking to her, not even looking at her. Tabitha couldn't afford to lose her fucking job over this. She would need to talk to the flirter later, get him to match his story with hers. She had only been in the room a couple—no, five—five to seven minutes. Standard, with a little chit-chat. Nothing out of the ordinary. Unless they had already gotten to him first. Shit.

Without this job, she wouldn't be able to pay rent, groceries. Back to her old room at her mom's house, the one filled with extra boxes of Hamburger Helper because Mom was a little hoardery about Sam's Club bulk.

One of the residents, the cute one who always needed sleep and a comb, pushed out of the OR. Yawned, stretched his arms and laced his fingers behind his head. Over his shoulder, Loretta and the emergency docs and nurses that had crowded around Ginny now dispersed.

Tabitha seethed through her teeth. Cringed.

"Well," the resident said. "We got her back. Barely, but she'll make it."

The relief broke the tension. Tabitha's held-back tears spilled, smacked on the floor.

Then the resident said, "But she'll never be the same. Her brain went without oxygen for too long. What's left of her won't be able to do much. She'll pretty much be a toddler the rest of her life."

He went back in and Tabitha sat down. She wondered if there would still be enough left of Ginny Lafitte deep in her brain to think of this as the ultimate Hell. Still wanting to die, and no one to let her.

Horrible.

If Tabitha didn't lose her job over this, maybe she'd help the poor crazy bitch. One shot, nighty-night…

…No, she couldn't. What she could do was request a transfer to a new floor. Fuck this drama for good.

# CHAPTER ELEVEN

"Oh my God!"

It was all Melissa could do to keep from cumming. Squeezed her thighs together and widened her eyes while DeVaughn sped the fuck out of there in reverse, head turned over his shoulder, trying to keep Lafitte in sight.

"Shit!" He backed through the four-way stop, threw it into drive, and squealed a right turn. Steel on rock, screaming, probably the bumper getting sheared off. That goddamned bike had fucked up his car bad.

"Get him, baby! He went over there—"

"I saw where he went, shit! We're not going to get him here"

"He can't get far!" She pulled her legs beneath her and leaned her cheek against his shoulder. "I can shoot him out the window."

DeVaughn shook her off. "I got to drive, baby. We've got to get out of here and ditch this car."

"But you love your Caddy."

"I'll buy another one.

Melissa pouted a little, but she was too excited to give a shit right then. This was real! Heart-in-her-throat real! She was feeling the danger of it, the sex of it, like, being inside one of those Grand Theft Auto games her ex played. This was so much better. Best day of her life— great sex, lunch at a restaurant that cost a whole day's pay, riding in the Caddy with a real man who carried a real nine millimeter Glock, going after real revenge on a bad guy who had killed his brother. She wasn't even wearing her seatbelt. Even the bang on her head and the little gash on her leg was nothing. She didn't even feel it now.

They made it to Mobile as quick as they could, one of One Oh Four's soldiers calling in a Lafitte sighting outside the facility DeVaughn had told them about. So they relieved him and waited for Lafitte's little raggedy ass to come out. Best place for it. He'd been planning it ever since Lo-Wider turned him on to Lafitte being back around.

How the fuck did she get so lucky? If she ever made it back to the truck stop, although they would probably fire her for missing her shift later anyway, she would be sure to thank the manager for giving her the chance to get picked up by DeVaughn. It was fate and the late-shift.

Lafitte, the little truck driver's name, had been as polite as could be, and left her a decent tip. But what they always say is that the nice ones are the ones to watch out for. DeVaughn had told her the story, Lafitte and his partner lording around Gulfport like they owned the place, bullying themselves into a piece of BGM cash. Then, right after the storm, how they ended up assassinating DeVaughn's brother over this bag of heroin they'd found. Mind you, finding it was sheer luck. They found it in a casket in the back of an abandoned hearse. They needed someone to move it. The kid got himself in too deep, talked to the wrong people—in this case, the *good* cops—and there it was: a reason for the bad cops to get rid of DeVaughn's little brother.

If it made DeVaughn happy, then Melissa's new ambition in life was to kill this motherfucker.

"Over there," she pointed across the road, a corner used car lot, packed tight and surrounded by pine trees on one side, a closed-down Wendy's on the other. The joint had obviously been a gas station at one point. Too many pennant-flag strings, yellow and orange, criss-crossing, flapping. None of the cars were top-notch. What they were was *there*.

"Shit, baby, we don't have time."

"Sure we do. We've got this. Pull over in the Wendy's lot."

So he did, parking in back, the building hiding the car from a street view. He got out, shrugged his coat into place and buttoned it. Melissa pulled her dress down, smoothed it. She stretched out a hand to DeVaughn. *Come hither.* "Give me the gun."

DeVaughn looked around. Sirens still out there, bouncing this way and that. He shook his head, but with a little grin. "Shit. I'm going to have to get you your own."

"Right now, I want yours."

"I might need it. Come on." He stepped over, offered his arm. "Let's do this with class. You have a favorite?"

She took his arm and held her chin high. They stopped at the edge of the lot, standing on a concrete divider, scoping out the selection. The fat white "bro" in khakis and a golf shirt stood at the front window, watching, but probably thinking, "Not worth getting out in the heat for."

Most of the cars were nineties mid-range shit. Pontiacs, Chevies, some ass-ugly Dodge cars, goddamn.

Neon? Stratus?

Melissa tightened her grip on DeVaughn and then pointed toward the far corner. A real beauty—you had to see past the flaws, of course. A red Hyundai Tiburon had been left out in the sun too long, clear coat peeling on the top and hood. But, hey, sun-roof. Paint on the window said it had 96K miles and cost seven thousand and change. Had to be a joke. A joke so good, they laughed at it.

DeVaughn said, "Let's go get it."

They walked across the lot, the sunshine banging off metal and chrome and fiberglass. She pretended it was paparazzi flashes. Lost in the moment. DeVaughn's hand slid from hers, slid onto her ass, grabbing himself a squeeze. She did the same, slipping her fingertips into his slacks pocket. Feeling like a million fucking dollars, worth maybe seventy-five grand. The fat sales-bro backed off from the window, can of Cherry Dr. Pepper in his hand, resting against his paunch. They watched him huff, shake his head, then head outside.

"Doing alright?" he asked.

"Fine. How about yourself?"

"I'm here by myself today. Can't let you test-drive anything."

"Is that so?"

Shrug. "Wish I could. Try back tomorrow if you see something you want to drive." He gave Melissa a long look, up and down. DeVaughn could almost read the bro's mind: *the zits, but nice lips. The weight, but nice shape.* Starting to piss DeVaughn off because he knew what was next: *yeah, niggers like fat ugly white girls.*

Quicker than it took to get mad, Melissa's hand rose

from DeVaughn's pocket, up the back of his jacket to where he'd shoved the gun into his waistband, and tugged it once, twice, until it was free. She brought it up nice and smooth and pointed it between the sales-bro's eyes.

She said, "Go get me the keys for the red Tiburon."

Hands up, not even dropping the Dr. Pepper. "Hey, hey, hold on. Please. My boss. Please."

"Get me the keys."

Salesbro blinked a lot. DeVaughn wondered if he would do the same, someone pointing a gun at him. Wondered if his brother had when Lafitte and Asimov did that shit. Melissa held it like a girl, of course. Bit limp and flippy with it.

The problem with Salesbro was he was still trying to think his way out of this. DeVaughn stepped up to him—watched him go "No no no no!" and cower back—and grabbed the back of his neck, turned him right around back through the glass door into the shop. First thing DeVaughn saw was another guy peeking over a desk in the next room, wood panel walls with a Plexiglas window. He pointed so Melissa would see, and she turned her aim onto the new guy.

This one, sandy spiky hair, no sideburns. Jeans and a dress shirt, knit tie. Loafers and no socks. Hands sort of up, at his waist, because shit, he wasn't no coward, was he? He'd *dreamed* of this day, wasn't going to react like some people, just give away the store. Not when he had taken those ju-jitsu classes. No, he would—

Melissa shot him. Right through the Plexiglas. Surprised the goddamned living fuck out of DeVaughn, the shot shutting down his ears, making him flinch and lose his grip on the bro. Didn't matter, because the bro had probably shit himself. He dropped to the floor, curled up. Through the ringing, it sounded like he was crying. Melissa stepped into the office and squatted beside the guy she shot. Knees together, heels up off her flip flops. The gun dangled loose in her grip, over her knee. She watched, waited. A very patient killer. He must've moved or some shit, because she stood up and shot him again. Then she turned back to the bro.

Dude was all a mess. Sloppy and fat and useless. Melissa took her foot, asphalt-stained flip-flop and all, and pressed it on his cheek, going, "Sh, sh, shush. Sh, sh, shush."

When she had his attention, she said, "Red Tiburon. Keys. Now."

He climbed off the floor, still holding his Dr. Pepper, now crushed and oozing and all over his sleeve. Melissa palmed the back of his neck the way she might a lover, and she jabbed the gun into his gut. She didn't have to say anything. He nodded. He wheezed. They headed into the office where the other man lay dead on the floor.

DeVaughn looked away, out the front windows. It was a really nice day, maybe a little too hot, sure. It was always a little too hot most of the time. No breeze today.

Lafitte should've died when they hit him in the car. Should've died when DeVaughn shot at him. Shit, he should've died instead of DeVaughn's brother, is what he should've done.

Another gunshot.

DeVaughn spun round to watch Melissa do a Beyonce walk out of that office where there were now two dead men. She tossed the key and fob in the air, caught it again. "Ready?"

He held the front door open for her. He had to play catch up when she sashayed past.

"Girl? Goddamn! Someone had to have heard."

"I figured."

"You better walk a little faster, then."

"Ain't no need. I'm driving, too. I've always wanted a sports car."

"Jesus, baby, you even listening to me?" He grabbed her around the waist and pulled her to him and got up in her ear. "You just killed those motherfuckers."

She rested her cheek against his lips. "Look, you're the one told me you want Lafitte dead. Then you shoot at him like we're at the fair. Like you want to win me a stuffed monkey. Do you want to win me one of them?"

"Shit."

"I don't need monkeys."

"What you need?"

She grinned. Broke away from him and kept walking. "Look at this car! It's a fine-ass car."

"I said what you need, baby?"

She put her hands on her hips and twirled to face him. "I need you to get used to seeing dead guys if you want to kill Billy Lafitte. I need you to pull that trigger and mean it. Get in my car."

" *Your* car?"

"You wrecked yours, and I killed two white boys for this one, so yeah."

Unbelievable. He needed to take a big piss. But he wasn't going back into the little building behind them. He wondered if there were people watching from close-by, on their phones describing him and Melissa to the cops. He hoped they were saying *Fine suit, handsome motherfucker. Girl has got an ass she knows how to use.*

She opened the driver's door of the Tiburon, and DeVaughn went around, got in the other side. Hot as balls in the car. Waves of heat coming out as he sat down. She cranked up and revved and revved again. Turned the a/c on full, a blast of hot making them both cough first before the cold hit. He expected her to shift into gear, but first Melissa grabbed his crotch all the sudden and said, "If we weren't in a hurry, I would've let you fuck me back on the desk in their office."

"You serious? Dead guys watching and shit?"

"I feel you getting hard. You know you would've."

She was right. Off they went, too fast down a road lined with strip malls and fast food joints.

# CHAPTER TWELVE

An hour into the flight, the turbulence shook them hard. Rome closed his eyes, interlaced his fingers on his lap, and took a deep breath. "Airplane crash" was a more high-profile way to die than "hit a deer". Maybe people seeing his name on the victims list would get the nation talking about Lafitte again. Since he'd escaped and been able to stay escaped, the news had gotten tired of talking about it, and had stopped mentioning the sightings altogether.

Rome could be a martyr for his cause.

Worth it.

But when he opened his eyes after a calm stretch, the flight attendant was already up again, picking up the drink orders where he had left off. Nothing fancy, water or orange juice. Conventional wisdom: if the flight attendant is up and about, then no worries. This was a small jet, a CRJ-700, a bit stuffy but still plenty of leg room on the exit row they had paid extra for. Only four "first class" seats, only three taken this flight, both by lucky upgraders instead of someone who paid full price. He could tell because even back here, he heard word-for-word a conversation between a loud old woman and the flight attendant, telling him all about her upgrading adventures, and him doing a shit job pretending to care. Even *she* could tell the "sky waiter" didn't care, but that didn't stop her.

Wyatt read a magazine. Rome couldn't read on planes. Never could. Didn't like movies on flights, either. He listened to the drone of the engines, cringed to the slight bounce of the fuselage on the air currents. If he didn't concentrate on those things, it would all fall apart. His willpower was what held the plane together.

Another bitchslap of turbulence. Jesus! He had to grab hold of the headrest in front of him.

Wyatt said, "Hey, Frank, take a look," and started to pass over an article—some shit about an over-fifty dating service—but then the article was in his face, pressed hard against it. Rome reached up and grabbed the edge, peeled it off. He was disoriented. The plane's dinger went ding-dong four times, and the flight attendant said, "Excuse me," to the old woman as he turned for the phone, but the jolt came fast and dropped him to the ground as they lurched to the right. Way far right. Goddamn almost turned upside-down. People falling out of seats, luggage slamming down from the overheads. Screams.

Engines screaming too.

Oxygen masks.

Something cold. Cold all over. Smoke.

Ears pop pop popping.

Disembodied voices from the speakers: "Keep calm! Keep fucking calm! I can't—I can't—shit! I can't!"

Wyatt, grunting, white-knuckling the armrests.

Rome closed his eyes.

Still totally worth it.

# CHAPTER THIRTEEN

Lafitte took stock.

His elbow, a fucking bloody mess. Rubbed a patch of skin clean down to the bone. Ear was all skuzzed up from gravel, broken asphalt. Cheek, too.

But other than the blood, the burning, and the electric cattle prod his heart was turning into, he got out of it pretty fucking clean.

Behind a house in an old subdivision, all brick homes in one of three styles, propped against the back wall in a fenced yard with a colorful, plastic swing-set, an air conditioning unit, roaring, next to a water hose snaking through unmown grass. He turned it on a trickle, hoping no one inside would notice, and took a long drink before washing off the blood, dirt, and rocks.

DeVaughn had known where Ginny was, had he? Or had someone follow him there? Shit. DeVaughn knew too much. Shit. BGM and DeVaughn had been the ones writing in shit. Shit. Shit. How long had they known? By the time they wrote on the wall of the truck stop, it was too late. He'd already committed. Like a dog and bell, he came running. Shit. Is that all that was left in his skull? Shit? DeVaughn? Not Rome? Not the FBI?

"Shit."

The smell of shit all over the yard. Dog shit. He looked around—no dog. But then he heard it, the barking, relentless, scrabbling at the back sliding-glass door. He couldn't see it from his spot. Squeaking, squeaking, dog nails on glass. Relentless. Barking. But that was good, right? No one had come outside to see what the puppy was barking at. No one had yelled for it to shut up.

The electric cattle prod bit harder each time and took longer to fade away. He flexed the fingers on his left hand, even though he knew the pain wasn't in his muscles. Not those muscles, anyway. He had been sitting on his heels, back up against the house, tense all over, and finally stuck his feet out in front of him, ass on the ground. Relief.

First thing, he needed a car. There had to be plenty in this neighborhood, in garages or parked on the curb. Okay. Actually, it wasn't the first thing. The first thing was to stop hurting. He was holding his breath without thinking, trying to stop the pulsing, white-hot—

—Ginny, dead. Ginny, bruise around her neck. Smiling. Thanking him—

He must have dozed off. Not sure of the time. Maybe the sky was darker, or maybe it was his eyes still adjusting to the light. Someone out front on the street was revving their engine for fun. Then high-pitched brakes, then nothing. Was the dog still barking? The pain had subsided, mostly. He checked his elbow, his ear. Crusty blood, dry. Good.

He pushed himself off the ground, hand on top of the A/C unit until he was sure he could walk. There was a wooden backdoor, probably led to the garage. He crouched and duck-walked over to it, tried the knob. It was open. He pushed, but it only went another inch. Chain lock up top.

The energy leaked out of him and he ached all over again. But fuck that. He put his boot in the gap at the bottom, pressed hard with his knee, then shouldered the door, more pressure gradually, trying to keep the noise down. He was just under eye-level with the chain, watched as the screws holding the latch stripped out of the door frame. He stumbled inside the garage.

The door only opened forty-five degrees, blocked by plastic totes. Those and cardboard boxes and tools piled on wobbly steel shelves, five high, along with beat-to-shit and sun-faded toys the kids must've lost interest in. And, thankfully, a car, all packed into a narrow garage. He wondered if it meant there was someone home after all. But he couldn't hear anything except the dog still barking, whining, scratching, now at the interior garage door. Lafitte closed the back door, too dark, no windows in here, but then left it open a crack, enough to help him see as he walked sideways between a wall of boxes and the passenger side.

The car was a shitpile, no doubt. Tan, four-doors, what was this thing? Saturn. Yeah, Saturn. In the back window, a community college parking permit from 2003, half-gone from someone trying to peel it off. Lafitte nearly got hung up on the tow hitch—seriously? This thing could tow shit?—scooting between the rear to the driver's side. He opened the driver's door, sat down. The scent of sickly-sweet perfume nauseated him. The inside light showed a bunch of papers, school handouts, and empty Skittles bags, and a little stuffed clown hanging off the rearview by its arms, right beside a high school parking permit, this year.

A kid's car. A hand-me-down, or bought used.

Whatever. He checked for spare keys tucked into the visors, but yeah, no one did that much anymore. He needed to hotwire it. So, okay, he did. He hot-wired it, the perfume making him hungry for some reason, and then he tapped the garage door opener, put the car into reverse, and waited until the door was up.

Outside were two pick-up trucks across the street on the curb, parked nose-to-nose, a handful of guys, three shirtless, standing around, and one sitting in the driver's seat of a chopped-down GMC. They all stared at him.

Of course they did. Of course they would be there.

Then Lafitte looked at the house he'd been hiding behind. In the front window, a teenage girl, phone to her face, now shouting, easy to tell, and pointing. Then her face disappeared and a moment later she was outside, phone still to her face, shouting about, "He's stealing my car! My car!" Right behind her was the dog, a shaggy mutt, barking and running in circles.

The guys in the street—what, late teens? Twenties?—moved toward the driveway. Lafitte hadn't even cleared it yet. They blocked the path. One of the guys headed up to the passenger door and yanked the handle a few times. Pounded his palm on the window. "Stop the car, bitch! The cops are coming! Stop the car!"

Lafitte inched back some more. The guys blocking his way stepped forward and laid their hands on the trunk. The shirtless guy at the window was still slapping, still telling him, "We're not playing! Stop the fucking car! You're not taking her car!"

The girl had gotten brave enough to stand right behind the guy, phone still to her face.

Jesus. Couldn't Lafitte have *one* stolen vehicle for the

day without anyone fucking it up? If those idiots had just left his Muscle Max truck alone...

He let out a breath. Took his foot off the brake, punched the gas and the car jumped backwards. The guy on the side flinched away, same as two of the guys at the trunk, except one who got his feet tangled and went down and, goddamn it, Lafitte punched the gas again and must've gone right over the guy like a speedbump.

The teenage girl screamed and in the rearview was the whole fucking population of the street watching from their yards, with their phones up and recording, and these guys panicking over their friend under the back wheels.

Lafitte pulled the stick into drive and gunned it forward. The speedbump wasn't as easy this time. First two tries, it was like he was slamming into a concrete block. The other guys, waving their hands wildly in front of him, shouting "Shit! Fuck! No! God, no! Stop it! Stop it!"

Then the third time, the resistance gave way and he bounced up and over the body, and nobody stood in his fucking way this time. Lafitte looked in the rearview and saw all of these people running toward whoever he had run over. He couldn't see the body itself, surrounded now, but he did see the trail of red tire-tracks starting nice and wide and bright back at the house, fading as he put distance between himself and the scene.

He hoped the guy would be okay.

He needed another car. Something easier this time.

\* \* \*

It took two more carjacks to get a clean one. Finally. Someone left a Mitsubishi running outside a Target because they'd left a dog inside. Yappy little shit. Schnauzer. He looked at the tag on its collar—Kaiser. Then the names Lynn and Chris and two phone numbers. It was probably chipped. They couldn't track it, right? Lafitte thought of letting the little thing out into the parking lot, but fuck, he was lonely.

After seeing Ginny, hoping she'd found some peace at last, the next impulse drew him north again, back to Minnesota, where all the bad things had happened—but it wasn't as strong a pulse as before. His head was beginning to clear and he was getting through the fog. He had unfinished business.

Kaiser the Schnauzer settled after a few minutes of growling. Lafitte laid his hand on the dog, now curled in the passenger seat. Stroked his fur. DeVaughn had engineered this shit somehow, so maybe Lafitte needed to see it through. He'd always have someone behind him—the FBI, Homeland Security, Rome, Ginny's mom—but he couldn't lay blame on them. They were doing what they had to do. DeVaughn could've left well enough. He should've.

No, it was Lafitte himself. His own internal radar couldn't leave well enough alone. His whole life was a scab he kept picking, like walking into this trap—*you knew it was a fucking trap, you fucktard*—for the sheer hell of it, convinced no one could catch him now, not after prison. Not after watching his son die because of some stuck-up Christian bitch wanting to teach her grandson a lesson, and Colleen still ass-hurt over her dead husband, putting everyone at risk to make herself feel a little better.

So, fine, where's this busted radar going to lead you now? Where's this ego, leaking like a cracked nuke, going to steer us?

Well...there was this one guy. If Lafitte was going to square things with DeVaughn, he needed time to heal. And that meant squaring things with someone he hadn't seen in almost twenty years.

Lafitte ditched the car in a parking lot in Biloxi with broken asphalt and long wild grass growing knee-high between the cracks. There had once been a K&B Drugstore, but it had turned into some other chain and then another and then it had become a store for ethnic hair products that wasn't there anymore. A big grocery store had centered the place, also gone. He remembered it had been closed long before Katrina. The water mark from the storm was still high on the wall all these years later, next to the graffiti from the Coast Guard marking how many dead were found here—six. But down the line, business was alive if not well. A Chinese take-out, and two check cashing joints. Yep, two of them, not even fifty yards apart.

He found a leash for Kaiser in the backseat, and he even locked the Mitsubishi's doors with the keys still inside, engine running. Maybe it would run out of gas before someone else came along and re-stole it, but Lafitte doubted it. Eight minutes, tops. The thief, whoever it turned out to be, was probably watching him right now, making sure it wasn't a "cop drop" to lure a rat to the cheese, same as Lafitte coming close to getting his own neck snapped by DeVaughn. But it didn't matter. At least one rat would still take the bait, God bless him. Today that car thief would get away with it for a while.

The heat. It was the first chance he really had to enjoy the heat again. Clear sky, the sun piercing enough to make him squint, but the asphalt below soaking it up, then steaming it back at him. The sweat was a relief. Kaiser had no idea where they were going, but he led anyway, past the shopping center into an older neighborhood, past an apartment complex built in the eighties, looking as run down as a French Quarter warehouse from the eighteenth century.

It had been, what, fifteen? Twenty years? Hadn't been down this street in nearly twenty years, and then only the one time. He had ended up having to get help from this guy buying a car, and was embarrassed to need it. Lafitte had written the guy off before then, and it wasn't like he'd made an effort to come see Billy on his own. Maybe he didn't even live back here anymore. It was a stab in the dark.

The neighborhood was deeper than Lafitte remembered. Quiet out, too hot for a lot of outdoors stuff. Only one kid mowing. He heard splashing from a backyard. Probably an inflatable pool. The grass was dying in too many yards, reminding him of fall in Minnesota, except here it was from drought. The heat was like a goddamned jungle. Every step, he watched waves of hot air rise from the ground ahead of him. Jesus, it was making him sleepy.

The house he was looking for, right where it used to

be, where it had always been. It was brick, red. A ranch style. A one car garage, a little gated courtyard leading to the front door. In the driveway, and angled across the lawn, two cars—one Chrysler 300, and a Lincoln, early '00s. Lafitte stopped to let Kaiser piss on the lawn before heading up to the door. All around the courtyard, ceramic frogs and a fish spitting water into a ceramic pond, a bench too small to sit on, but it didn't matter because two potted plants, no flowers, took up all the space. Lafitte twisted the leash around his hand because he didn't know what to expect, what races this dog might or might not like. He stabbed at the doorbell, a heavy, seventies ring to it, and then propped his arm on the doorjamb, asleep on his feet.

The door swung open, and the cool air was a revelation. The man standing there, another twenty years lining his face, well past sixty now. Puffy cheeks, acne-scarred chin and forehead, skin light brown. He still wore his hair swooped back, blow-dried, one big pomp with high sheen to it, but the darkness was a dye job, had to be. Lafitte remembered the old man had taken to *Miami Vice* in the eighties, Don Johnson's signature look. It looked as if had anchored himself to it ever since.

Otherwise, he had a small beer gut, still had strong arms, shown off in a too-tight turquoise polo shirt, and he still wore a gold chain with a sailor's cross. His jeans were perfect, a crease ironed into them, and on his feet were moccasins and no socks.

The look on his face, a little blank at first, before his eyes widened and he opened the door all the way.

"Son?"

111

Kaiser was cool with him, so Lafitte felt a big sense of relief and brushed past the old man's shoulder into the house, heading for the nearest place to sit his ass down. He said, "I'm not your son, Manuel."

# CHAPTER FOURTEEN

DeVaughn washed his hands in the Waffle House sink and splashed a little on his face. Someone had tried the door knob and was now shuffling around out there, getting impatient, so DeVaughn slowed down. Make the fucker wait.

Eyes were red. Mouth was dry.

Shit, Melissa, man.

First, she was fucking crazy. He could tell from fucking her, but that was a good kind of fucking crazy. That was what all boys who've ever watched porn hoped for in a woman.

But, second, she was fucking crazy. Jesus, slapping gangstas and straight up murdering car salesmen, calm about it. Girl had devil eyes. Girl got off on killing. Girl wanted to fuck on top of bodies.

He dried his hands slowly, then his face. He opened the bathroom door. Fat white man in a beard and trucker cap turned like he was all mad, then looked away quick. Yeah, he'd better. DeVaughn stood in the open doorway an extra moment to piss the guy off more. Then made his way out through the swinging door to the dining room, smacked in the face with the smell of greasy eggs, greasy steaks, and old coffee. All Waffle Houses were the same. A few booths lined the kitchen, then the counter and stools, then a few more booths against the far windows, where his people were slumped all over everything. BGM soldiers on loan, none of them had real cred yet, some of them still in baggy jeans, the whole trend like clown pants now, DeVaughn thought. Six in all. Manspreading in the booths, and a couple barely staying on top of theirs stools, one on each side of Melissa. She turned left and right, left and right, lazily, ankles crossed, elbows on the counter, stirring a straw in her Mountain Dew.

At least Lo-Wider was there, too, relieved the cops had found his grampa's Monte Carlo unharmed thanks to a security guard at a rest area. So he wasn't so glum anymore. He was chowing down an omelet and grits. He was the only one eating. In fact, except for Melissa and Lo-Wider, no one else had even ordered. They'd all brought in their own bottles of Mountain Dew or tall boys of energy drink. The manager, he could tell, didn't like this shit, and she kept glancing over, not ready to say it yet but close.

The kid on the stool to Melissa's right was new. Saying, "Nigga *killed* his *wife*? Shit, why we chasing him, then?"

"He killed my brother, too. Good enough for you?"

Oh, snap, the soldiers giggling themselves into fits as new boy ducked his head and was all, "Shut up, bitches."

The manager was now right near DeVaughn, on the opposite side of the counter. Tall, thin, white, and older. She had a man's face if that man looked like a horse. Crossed arms. Cleared her throat.

DeVaughn sighed and pulled out his roll, peeling off forty and handed it over. "Whatever they want, on me."

He sat in the booth opposite Lo-Wider, sideways and on the edge because the boy's legs were trunks filling all the available space. The two on the stools plus Melissa turned his way. All the others, leaning closer.

"I don't know where he is. What we need from you is to find him."

Nothing.

"I mean, you know, some research or some shit. Hasn't he still got a kid living around here? Or some sort of family? Something?"

"Thought you were gonna tell us." One of the energy drinkers.

"What are you saying?"

The kid held his can so it covered his mouth, as if he was going to take a sip any second. "Like, didn't expect homework."

DeVaughn gave him a hard eye, hard as he could muster anymore. Poker made his eye look a lot less dangerous, a lot more *I know what you're holding*, but these BGM's, they didn't even know what they were holding. It didn't much work at all. "You know, if you've got something else to do."

One of the others, named YP for some reason, said, "Boy doesn't want to say he has a hard time with long words, like *the* and *what*."

They busted laughing, and white people eating looked all mad. Made DeVaughn grin, shake his head.

It was Melissa who got them calmed. Reclined on the counter, arms resting on it, crossed her legs so the one on top was mighty high and her toe pointed and all Beyonce.

She said, "You've got to look up his whole name.

William Lafitte. Middle name was, what was it, DeVaughn?"

DeVaughn told her.

"Right, yeah. Look it up."

A few were already on their phones doing it.

DeVaughn gave her a look. "Thank you, baby."

She smiled. He got warm.

YP was like, "Hold up, hold up, how old is he?"

"About, what, forty? Thirty-eight?"

"You heard if his mom's dead?"

DeVaughn shrugged. Shit, he thought he knew this guy inside and out. Now he wondered if he'd really cared that his brother had died after all. Wondered if he gave a shit about revenge or if it was just obligation.

"Let me see."

YP got up, showed his phone to DeVaughn. An obituary for Lafitte's mother. Well, goddamn. A list of survivors.

DeVaughn winked at Melissa, towering over him right now like she was on a throne. Being a Queen came naturally to her. Too bad everyone else couldn't see past the cellulite to realize.

"Finish up your drink," he told her. "We've got someplace to be."

# CHAPTER FIFTEEN

The afterlife sure enough sucked.

If that was what this was, anyway. Rome couldn't figure out if time was passing or stopped or happening all at once. There would start to be a dream, maybe a dream, people he knew but who didn't look like themselves, or sound like themselves, and then the scene would cut out and he would forget it instantly. Then a song, pounding, hitting him on the head like a bottle. Then, what, "Sir? Sir? Can you hear me? You're going to be alright."

From all around. From different voices. Cold then hot then salty then bitter.

Then it would start again.

And the fucking pain, shit, as if pain was everywhere. No body to pinpoint it on—left, right, up, down, pain pain pain the pure essence of pain—

This was Hell, the literal Hell of the Bible, the goddamned—he shouldn't say that word, it was a blasphemous word, but if he was in Hell it was too late to blaspheme or repent or fuck it's too HOT it's too COLD it's too TOO.

But then he forgot what he'd felt and there was another dream and he forgot his first dream and then it was TOO TOO TOO...

\* \* \*

117

Time came back in strange ways. He was lifted up and set down again. It made him blink, made him see lights. People. Faces. Masks. Surgeons? One hovering, She was shoving something painful and plastic into his mouth. He tried to speak to her but all that came out were rocks and brake squeals.

"Oh my god, he's awake!"

Then he forgot and there was another dream where he was having trouble talking to his wife. He was mad at her for something, maybe for dying, and wanted to shout at her but all that came out were more rocks, more brake squeals. She stood there with that face, the one the mortician reconstructed after the bullet had wrecked most of her first one, lips curling, finally saying, "Least I tried."


Rome was back in his cabin, although it seemed jittery, out-sized, as if the lake was rolling in right at his feet. He was sitting in his favorite chair, watching out the same windows. Gray skies, lamplight beside him. Next to him, in the chair no one ever sat in because he never had visitors, was Billy Lafitte. This was the Lafitte of when they had first met, Billy as an arrogant deputy-sheriff in Yellow Medicine County with a Gene Vincent pomp and a Johnny Cash sneer.

Lafitte said, "So where do we go from here?"

"Will they let me chase you across Hell?"

"Ask me again once we're dead."

"Hard to tell."

"What about him?" Lafitte jerked a thumb at the windows. On the outside, lying on the glass as if it was horizontal, not vertical, was the wrecked, limp body of Wyatt. Not a complete view of him. More like a close-up.

"He's dead."

"You know for sure?"

"I think I do."

Lafitte stood. He was carrying a mug of coffee. He walked over to the window, sipping and staring as if Wyatt's corpse was not blocking the view. "You still know live from dead. You saw this," he indicated Wyatt with the mug. "Right before you went under. You know dead. You know you survived."

"Say I did. Now what?"

Lafitte turned. "I guess you and me can talk it out. I'll say the things you've always wanted me to say. You can kill me a bunch."

Headache. Rome rubbed his forehead. "It won't mean anything."

Shrug. "Something to pass the time, I guess."

He sat again. The lake was in the window once more, waves impossibly high, impossibly loud.

Rome looked down. He was holding a coffee mug, too. He couldn't read the writing on it. "I'm sorry, you know. I'm sorry I killed that girl of yours. The bass player."

"Drew. Her name was Drew."

"Yeah, if only...but it's your turn. Say you're sorry you killed my wife. Desiree."

Lafitte smiled wide. "Shit, she was going to shoot me. I'm glad I killed that bitch. I'm glad I shot her twice. You should know by now, the only time you'll get an apology from me is when I'm done with you."

\* \* \*

*He's flatlining. He's gone.*
*No! How the hell—*
*Wait, he's back.*
*Come on, Mister Rome, you survived a plane crash*
*already, so don't let me be the one to kill you.*

# CHAPTER SIXTEEN

Manuel fed Kasier half a can of cat food. Dogs don't care. Dogs eat anything. Manuel put it in a bowl and set it at Lafitte's feet. Kaiser started into it and pushed the bowl all the way to the wall.

Manuel sat beside Lafitte at the small round table in the kitchen, one made of aluminum with a vinyl top over cotton, stapled to fiberboard. It was dusty and covered in piles of unopened mail. Lafitte used a pile to prop up his elbow and his fist to prop up his face. Goddamn he was tired.

Manuel asked him if he wanted tea. Lafitte said no, but Manuel got him some tea anyway. Iced, too sweet, too weak.

"Your mother will love to see you."

Lafitte shook his head. "She's not my mother."

"Well..." Manuel picked at a spot where the cotton was stringing out of the vinyl. "She still calls you son, I mean. That's her way."

"My mother is dead. Your wife is nuts."

"And I let you in my home? With some dog? Not even a call after how many years?"

The dog had found the cat's water bowl and was lapping as much as he could. Across the kitchen on the counter was a small flat screen TV, a talk show, one of those "You *are* the father!" things. The sound was low. The TV looked out of place, too modern for this kitchen, but Lafitte thought even a flat screen was old these days. Most people would use their iPads. Hell, even their tiny-ass phones.

Lafitte closed his eyes. "I'm sorry, Manuel. I'm sorry. It's been a bad, you know, decade."

"I've kept up. Don't think I haven't."

"Is that a threat?"

Manuel reached across the table and gripped Lafitte's hand. "All these years. It's good to see you. It's really good. If you really thought I would turn you in, you wouldn't have come. Right? Son? I need to know."

Lafitte closed his eyes again, tighter, and tried to tug his hand away from Manuel's, but the old man wouldn't let go. Lafitte said, "All right, yeah, I know. I need help, man."

It was a strange feeling, this thing, this lump in Lafitte's throat. He hated Manuel. After his father had left or died or whatever, it was all a blur. His mother had bought a car from Manuel and then had a whirlwind romance that led to six shitty years of marriage, most of them forgotten now except for the parts where Manuel was either unfailingly generous but melodramatic—wanting Lafitte to call him 'Dad', getting his feelings hurt when Billy refused—or unfailingly drunk and almost violent. He never got quite to the point of hitting, choking, kicking. He would get loud and stupid. He would break things. The police had to be called a few times, but they knew Manuel and either gave him a warning and a ride to a motel, or a night in the drunk tank, until his mother had had enough and moved out, not even telling Billy where she was going. Billy and all his things, left behind. So Billy lived there for most of the year until he graduated high school and was able to move to a dorm for college. After that, "home" was either his grandmother's house, or wherever he happened to be sleeping.

He would see Manuel now and then, but tried to avoid him. Then Lafitte's mother died, and he found himself having to let Manuel come to the funeral with his new wife in tow. She was a kind woman, a Mexican who barely spoke English. Jimena. She was twelve years younger than Manuel, but with a shock of premature gray hair. While Billy had to agree with his other relatives that bringing her was bad taste, he couldn't help but notice how kind she was. How gentle. How she had the ability to do what his mother couldn't do—rein in Manuel's fire.

Lafitte said, "How is Jimena? Everything okay?"

"She's good. She'll be happy to see you."

"Me too." Tried to grin. "Hey, you don't know how to get me some nitro pills, do you?"

They heard a hiss and then a bark. The dog was gone. Manuel stood and rushed out, saying, "Blanco! No, leave the doggie alone! Blanco!"

Not the other way around.

Manuel always was a bullshitter.


He didn't realize he'd fallen asleep. Manuel had left him in a front sitting room, the pretty furniture for the priest or the neighbors should they visit. No TV. Lafitte had leaned back on the loveseat, then the dog had jumped up beside him, and the afternoon sun had angled so it was a little darker in here.

But before, while Manuel had locked the cat into another room, Lafitte had wandered out into the backyard. There was more stuff out here than there used to be. A wooden deck, that was new to Lafitte, even if it was old and weathered by now. Lots of flowerbeds, a chain-link fence on two sides lined up to the neighbor's plastic or privacy fence. It used to be all chain-link, so when he was out here with friends, or even out here alone, the neighbors' dogs on three sides would bark at him a while, then forget he was there, then bark again if he moved or made any noise. So he'd yell back at them and then the neighbors would yell from their windows and he'd yell at those fuckers and then dogs would bark some more.

He had fucking hated living here.

Manuel came outside, stood by him. "Are you feeling all right?"

"Listen. So. I, um, I helped Ginny kill herself. I think."

"Ah, boy. Boy. Jesus." A gush of breath. "Why did you tell me? Why would you *do* that?"

"She kept trying, years and years, and I finally saw her, and she asked me to. She wrote me letters. She was begging."

Manuel put a hand on Lafitte's shoulder, but Billy walked out from under it. Manuel said, "Are the kids okay?"

He wanted to punch the old man. Rage on him. But of course Manuel didn't know about Ham's death. How could he know? Mrs. Hoeck had kept Lafitte's whole side of the family from them, their cousins and great uncles and aunts. The authorities had managed to keep it quiet because heads would roll, right? Heads would roll. But somehow, someone was going to slip one day and it would be all over the news. Just not yet. So the step-grandparents sure as holy hell wouldn't know.

"Ham's dead. I watched him die."

"Jesus." Silence. "Jesus. What are you...what did you..."

Billy barked a laugh that got a dog barking too through one of the slatted fences. "I didn't do it, asshole."

"You can laugh about it?"

He turned. "Laughs aren't always happy. I saw him die and it was bad. He died bad. I couldn't stop it. It was all my fault. So I laugh. I laugh because I'm fucked."

"Billy, please."

"Please what? Now you know I broke out of prison, you know my kid died. I told you I helped kill Ginny. But I'm not here to kill you, so keep it together."

"I never thought you would."

"Sure, sure, because me and you, we were good. I was the teenage kid of the woman you were fucking. You got drunk and treated me like shit. You once peed in my parakeet's cage in the middle of the night. I once had to go out my bedroom window and get the neighbors because you were tearing apart our kitchen."

"Long time ago, buddy. Long time."

"But I don't know you now. That's all I ever think of you as. I'm never going to get over what you were. I shouldn't have to."

"Your mother, she forgave me."

"That's not the fucking point." He turned, got in Manuel's face. "You're all I've got, and I hate you. My son is dead. My wife is dead. I don't want to go anywhere near my girl because, yeah, because it's better if she never knows me. And now I'm here. I'm here. I need help. My chest hurts. I'm a fugitive. I've got nowhere else to go after this. And, fuck, I *hate* you. Can you tell me something that makes any sense? Anything? Anything that's not about me having to forgive you right now?"

He backed off. One step, two steps, three steps. Nearly tripped. Kaiser's paws scrabbling at his shins.

Manuel, Jesus, all sainted now. Hands clasped behind his back, a calm like Billy'd never seen from him. Fuck forgiving him. The guy didn't need it. He'd already found his peace or whatever shit it was in Spanish, what, *de paz interna? Que?*

Then Manuel led him inside, saying, "Get some ice water in you. You're dehydrated." Got him a glass. And within ten minutes Lafitte was on the loveseat, fading out.

Next thing he knew, he awoke to a woman's voice and a slamming door. His left arm was scrunched up, his hand a claw on his chest, and it was numb. Kaiser was curled on top of him, making it hard to breathe. And then Jimena was in the doorway, a continuous stream of Spanglish, shooing the dog off Lafitte, then out of the room, where it turned and peeked back.

"No doggie on the furniture. I don't like the dogs! I don't. You never call, you never visit, but then I'm expected to feed and clean up dog poops? You clean up your own dog poops, Billy. It's your dog."

She wore shorts. Her legs were tanned, shimmering, but some veins were showing through. Her shirt was thin, flowing, and sweat-through. After chasing the dog out, she came back, sat beside Lafitte, helped him sit up. An awkward hug, least on his end, as she squeezed and let the Spanish take over.

Then, "You stay, then? I wash these clothes for you? Billy, they say bad things about you, but family is family. My husband's son is my son, you see? We need to buy some food for the dog. Why did you bring a dog?"

"I'm not his son, you know—"

"We don't get to choose our families." Then her hands on his cheeks. "Look at you! What happened! A fight? You need some stitches, I do them. Did you get blood on the loveseat? Did you get any on the floor?"

This was the way he remembered her, mouth always going. Except that one time. That one time at his mother's funeral, she was the epitome of reverence. She was perfect. And he'd always been grateful for it. Looking at her now, the age having gathered on her in a graceful way, like Spanish moss on an oak. Her dark hair, long, a bit of a flyaway mess, shot through with more gray now.

He said, "Thank you. Thanks for everything."

Shrugged. "Where is this thanks coming from? Look, go away, puppy! No, not in this room. Off limits!" She turned back to Lafitte. "Go, go, go get a shower and take off those clothes. You need them? Is this real, this Muscle Max? I'm sure Manuel has...you're only a bit shorter is all."

She was up and off again, echoing through the house, shouting at Manuel, him shouting back. Not angry shouting, just shouting. Whatever. She was always kind to him, and she did know when to stop for breath.

He had fallen asleep right in front of the large picture window, in full-view of the entire street. He was letting his guard down, a bad thing to do. Outside, sunshine, an old-fashioned suburban street, kids riding bikes, skateboards, people in their yards, some iced tea and a cigarette, the smell of someone grilling steaks.

A whimper. Lafitte turned his head. Kaiser, still peeking in from the dining room. He wondered how long the owners had been frantically looking for him, how long it took them to realize the car was missing. He wondered if the guys he'd seen around the parking lot where he left the car would rat him out to cops—the white dude walking a dog? A little dog? Yeah, we saw. He was walking yo mama, too.

"Come on, buddy." He stood from the couch. "Let's get that shower."


There was a point during the shower, which pushed the pain in his arm and chest and jaw onto the back-burner, when Lafitte didn't want to ever get out. He was up for standing there and letting the hot water jet beat down on him twenty-four-seven. But really, right? Come on. What he needed to do was get himself back to full strength, get himself back to Minnesota, and from there, get lost in the northwoods like those off-grid types. Whole hell of a lot of them in Alaska, for sure. So many they've got TV shows. Kind of defeats the purpose, Lafitte thought.

But if DeVaughn would still be out there searching, stirring up trouble, could Lafitte feel safe? Having the entire U.S. Government was bad enough. At least

DeVaughn was just one guy. Crashing into him with his Cadillac was one way to go. Why do that? Why take the risk? Why so public, risk arrest? Something to do with the fat girl he was with. Something about her. That angry fat girl.

He looked at his scrapes and bruises. He rubbed over the crust of one, brushed the scabs off and watched the water run red. He grinned. He shouldn't have grinned. It made him think of Ginny. He shouldn't be grinning because Ginny was probably dead and he had helped. He had made it possible.

Did Manuel and Jimena already know? Wouldn't the cops have put out a net? Manuel was the closest thing to a parent he had left. Maybe they already knew and were being all nice in order to keep him here, keep him calm, make him forget the SWAT team was on the way. Jesus. Had he really lost his edge? Really?

He cranked off the water and slung the curtain open. Nothing there but Kaiser, curled up on the fluffy mint green rug, and a pile of fresh clothes, Manuel's, on the mint green toilet lid cover. Beside the toilet, a pair of beat-to-shit work boots. Black.

Lafitte toweled off, climbed out. He rubbed the fog from the mirror, but it fogged right back up. He stared into it, rubbed it clear again. Another stare. Dude was *beat the shit up*. As if the last four, five years hadn't fucked up his face and body enough. Dude looking back at him was a different dude. Dark bags under his eyes, one eyelid floppier than the other, hollow cheeks, scars on top of scars, skin all patchy, zits on the sides of his nose and on his chin. Stupid fucking mullet hair, streaky from where he'd dyed it to stay incognito. His neck was getting old before its time, too.

Hand though his hair, slinging water. Kaiser got up and shook off. Lafitte looked around. Some electric clippers on the back of the toilet. Okay, okay, that was something. He clicked them on and off a few times, then went after his sides, wild and frayed, covering most of his ear. He wanted it gone, hated his hair this way. Left, right, then an appraisal in the mirror. Okay, cool, okay. Now the mullet. He lowered his head and held his arm up and over and tried to do the best he could. Hard to tell. Guided the clippers up until they bumped and buzzed against his fingers. Sorry for fucking up the floor. Some was falling on Kaiser, too. But when he was done, he found a compact with a mirror in it and got the best view of the back of his head and saw it was good. Clean. He went over it again once more for strays. Then, very clean.

Now, what was left was all of this shaggy shit falling over his eyes. He thought about letting it all go, too, but thinking about Manuel for a second, he shook his head, searched in the medicine cabinet. There it was, as he guessed. A jar of Tres Flores Brilliantine. Some real greaser shit, only four bucks a jar, what all the *vatos* wore, and their fathers, and their grandfathers. It would do for now. Lafitte dug out two big licks, smoothed them in his palms until he had a hot grease smear, and slicked his hair back. Felt good. Felt like home.

Where there was grease, there had to be a comb. He clinked around some more in the medicine cabinet and found it, cleaned the leftover gray hair from it, wondered if it was Manuel's or Jimena's, then worked up a nice little pomp, the kind he used to wear. Gene Vincent. Unruly mop on top threatening to fall apart at the least urging, slicked back everywhere else. Made him want to howl. Made him want to punch someone, in a good way.

Now, this fucking beard.

Twenty minutes later, he stepped out of the bathroom, a sheepish left to right. No one. Wearing Manuel's jeans, rolled on the bottom. Boots. White T-shirt. Fuck, what if those two women in the Gospels had seen *this* walk out of Jesus' tomb, right?

He walked through to the kitchen, liking the heavy sound of his boots on the floor. He found Manuel sitting at the little table, staring into space, his hand wrapped around a Coors Light. No, not staring into space. The little TV on the counter. It was on one of the news channels, a plane crash. Then Manuel looked over at fresh-scrubbed Billy. "Now that's more like it. The Billy I remember."

"Yeah, beat to shit."

Waved him off. "The least of your worries. Beer's in the fridge." Then back to the TV.

Lafitte crossed to the fridge, got a beer, snapped it open and tried to block out the sound of the news guys. He'd heard enough of news, checking for his name on the national shit for a week or two after he had busted out. Once it had died down, there were still some local stories, sightings, but the tediousness of waiting for them to get to it got to him and he stopped bothering. Hated "news voice."

He sat beside Manuel. Had they ever sat down together with some beer? Ever? "Where's Jimena?"

"Out to get us pizza."

"They deliver, you know."

"Not from where we get it. Listen, now, hush and listen." Pointing at the TV.

Lafitte didn't want to. Took a cold drag of beer instead. But something familiar in the air, some sound. That thing where you hear your own name but no one's calling you. "What's going on?"

"Plane crash." Manuel raised his eyes. "Might be a friend of yours on the plane."

What now? What could it possibly be now?

"I don't have any friends."

"Sit, sit."

Lafitte sat and watched TV with his stepdad. Ex-stepdad. When they showed Franklin Rome's name and photo, it got him in the gut. He broke down, head between his knees, eyes burning. Manuel asked him what was wrong, and Lafitte finally got it out: "I'm free."

But he knew deep down it wasn't true and it would never be true, and he was even sad in a way, thinking about Rome out of his life, the way Batman must have been sad putting away the Riddler, the sorry fuck.

Then Manuel said, "No wait, he survived."

Well, goddamn it. Good news, bad news.

# CHAPTER SEVENTEEN

Melissa realized she hadn't had a cigarette all day. And she wasn't sure she wanted one now. DeVaughn's cock was better than Nicorette.

But, hey, if this BGM soldier was offering, who was she to say no? It was different than the usual cooling rush she felt blowing out a long stream of smoke on break from the truck stop, or after a fight with her jackass ex (yes, officially an ex now, for sure) when she'd been able to crush his fire under her heel like a cigarette butt. It felt good to win. She loved winning. She felt sexier. She'd killed two men for DeVaughn. They had cowered before her. Even better than fighting with the ex. The only time that hickster had treated her with any respect was when she'd turned on the sexy-bitch routine, lit up one right in the trailer, then promised him he wouldn't get any more of her pussy, and then talked about the black guys she'd been with. But her first cigarette after her first kills was better. Much better.

DeVaughn didn't take a cigarette. Not adamant or anything. A simple, "I'm good."

She asked him if he smoked, and he shrugged. "Playing poker? Sometime you've got to sit for hours and hours. Being around thick clouds of smoke for that many hours fucks up your throat and nose. And then sometimes, at tournaments, they don't let you smoke at all. So, shit, I gave it up by accident."

Good answer. He sure enough didn't seem to mind that she had smoked. Didn't seem to mind once they'd gotten down to it, her breath was all cigarettes and her stink was all cigarettes and grease and sweat. That was love. Love was not minding each other's smells. Him, all coffee breath and garlic. Some sort of body wash, Old Spice? One of those new Old Spices? And when he was done fucking her, his cum smelled sweet like hard candy.

DeVaughn sent YP—she wanted to call him "Yip", and he'd been giving her vibes, too, like, baby, once your man ain't around—and Lo-Wider off to check out Lafitte's stepdad's house, and the other soldiers to get strapped and ready for war. Lafitte was a living Stallone movie.

It left them alone again after her cigarette. Alone and bored. Bored was the big bad wolf. She hadn't been bored for nearly a full day and she didn't want it to end. So her being bored meant she got horny and pretty soon her and DeVaughn were in a Sonic Drive-In restroom where she sat on the toilet, sucking him off, except he was only getting a little hard and she started to worry he was bored, too. Was he already losing interest? Not love after all? Another goddamned misfire in her brain? She *knew* it was love, though, she *really knew it* this time. So she got into it even more, got her hand stroking harder, got her mouth more wet, used her tongue.

And when that didn't work, she started talking dirtier: "Want to fuck my ass? Want to cum in my ass? Don't you want to?"

And he sighed and laid his hands on her shoulders. "Look at me."

Cock still in her mouth, she did.

"It's okay, girl. It's okay. I've got a lot on my mind right now. It's not you, I swear."

He backed up, turned and zipped. She wiped her mouth with the back of her hand, stared at the drain in the floor. "Okay."

Tired of her. Or just plain tired. Or something.

Another minute of them being quiet. Then DeVaughn said, "Baby, when this is over, you and me, we can go anywhere we want. There are some tournaments in Florida. There are some up in Connecticut. Or, shit, up in Tunica all the time."

"Florida would be nice. I like Pensacola. I went to Panama City for Spring Break my junior year."

"Yeah. Florida. You know it. Soon as we take care of this. Soon as that Lafitte motherfucker is dead."

He sounded like he didn't believe it. Sounded like he thought they'd be in jail, like she'd gone and thrown the whole plan into the blender, killing those car guys.

She stood and walked over to him, put her palms flat on his back and leaned in close. Chin on his shoulder. "You mad?"

He let out a ragged breath. "At you? No, baby, no."

"Tell the truth."

"I didn't know."

"Didn't know what?"

"You got turned up over that. I don't know. I mean, I want to kill this motherfucker, no doubt about it, but, I didn't think...what I mean..." Wiggling now, popping one fist into his other hand. "One and done, you know? Didn't think there would be collateral damage."

"Don't call it that."

"What?"

"Collateral damage is what army dudes say to make it like they ain't killed the wrong people. What *you* need to say is they were *necessary* kills. What I did was get rid of two witnesses."

"Shit, girl, we left my car next door! They're gonna know! And we need to get Lafitte done with so we can get the hell out of here."

"Florida?"

"The fuck was I thinking, Florida? If we're lucky, we can hop a flight to France or or or Cabo or something. We can't go to Florida. Shit, unless we plan on swimming to Cuba after."

She swung DeVaughn around by the shoulders. "Look at me. I'm good. Paris. We do this, we go to Paris, you teach me to play cards, and we kiss this shitty country goodbye."

He shook his head, blinked a lot. "It's not that easy."

"It is. You got credit cards. You got a bank account. I did you a favor."

He couldn't help but grin. "Aw, goddamn. What is it about you?"

Someone started banging on the door. "'Scuse me?"

Melissa shouted, "I'm sick! I got diarrhea! Going to be awhile!"

Then she bit her lip and lowered her chin and took DeVaughn by the hands. "Come on, come here."

"What, baby?"

"Come here."

She pulled him over to the toilet, gave him a shove and sat him down. She pulled up her dress slowly. "Your turn."

"I said I'm not in the mood." But he was still grinning.

"Who gives a shit if you're in the mood?" Dress above her waist, she shoved the thin material of her panties aside, fingered her pussy. Went knuckle-deep with her middle finger. Moaned. "What mama wants, mama gets, and we'll worry about you later."

"Aw, Melissa, you ain't being fair."

She pulled out her finger and forced it into his mouth, past his teeth. "Fair? You think it's fair to leave me hanging? Or do you want me to go let one of the cute BGM niggas loosen me up first? Give you time to think about what's fair."

His eyes widened. Tried to talk around her finger. "*Bee-th.*"

"I'm sorry, I didn't get that." She curled her finger on top of his tongue.

"Oo. In-*saith*-a-bull."

She straddled him, started rubbing her crotch on his. "Let's get these pants wet. See how you like it."

Because it didn't matter if he was in the mood or not. She would make sure as fuck he wasn't *bored.*

# CHAPTER EIGHTEEN

Rome wasn't dead. That didn't make him feel any better.

Wyatt was, but Rome had only figured it out from what they weren't telling him. They weren't talking to him much at all, and when they did, as if he was an infant. Worse, an old man. Worse still, a middle-aged man who must look to them like a mentally-damaged pity case.

He tried to speak. Knew the nouns, verbs, adjectives, conjunctions, and even the right tones to signify questions, demands, sadness, anger. But when he tried to make them go from head to mouth, it was spit, drool, and some sort of honking. Like retarded people. Shit, he *was* retarded people.

If not, he would've said *I'm a fucking FBI agent. I was with fucking Homeland Security. I almost had Lafitte dead to rights. I was out there saving your asses from terrorism while you were still in high school, before you decided college was too hard and that a shitty less-than-one-year nursing assistant degree would be enough for you.*

Spittle. Drool. Could barely lift his hands to wipe it off, so he had cold drool all over his hospital gown and bandages, which most of the barely-nursing assistants ignored. On purpose. At first he thought it was because they knew what he thought of them. Then, because he was black. But the final realization was worse—they hated drool and hoped the next barely-nursing assistant would clean it up.

The crash was on TV. Some photos of him were in the rotation, official ones, a couple of candid ones from conferences or on vacation. Someone from Desiree's family must have handed those last ones over to the media. He wondered if there was a reporter in the hallway or waiting room hoping to see him. One of five survivors out of sixty-three. The co-pilot survived. A four-year-old survived. But a voice actor and a self-made multi-millionaire who owned a carpet franchise in eight states died.

Wyatt was dead. Desiree was still dead. Most likely, Rome's dream of dying alone in a cabin by the lake was dead, too. He might never be alone again, might need help to clean up his drool the rest of his life.

And he didn't dare ask why the blanket was flat next to his leg where the other one was supposed to be.

A knock on the already open door. He must have been standing there a few minutes already, but Rome hadn't noticed. He was too busy concentrating on the heart monitor, wondering if he could speed it up or slow it down at will. Just when it seemed to be working, something would make it jump or dip the wrong way.

Rome almost didn't recognize Shane Stoudemire, the man who had once been his superior at the FBI in New Orleans. Now he was, what, Rome couldn't remember. Climbing the administrative ladder, certainly. More than a Special Agent, more than a supervisor. The last time he and Rome had spoken had been after the shit had gone down at the prison, all the evidence pointing back to Rome. Got his ass chewed nice and royally. From this one, the royal dickhead. Fed Head. Rome wished, oh wished, the worst sort of sex scandal to take this piece of cow shit down.

Instead, here he was, standing in the doorway, a disgusted but polite smile on his face—Jesus, Rome needed a mirror—pretending to be concerned. Of course it was pretending. The guy had never shown a real emotion in his life, had he?

"Buddy? You awake over there? Have they got you on the good stuff?"

Rome stared. He wondered if they had told Stoudemire that Rome couldn't talk. Wondered if Fed Head would try to make him anyway. So Rome kept his mouth shut. Except he couldn't. Instead of the hard, silent stare Rome was going for, he had forgotten he was all neck-twisted, lips moving involuntarily, drooling, the sound of his breathing—wet steel wool.

Stoudemire walked to the end of the bed. He wore golf clothes, his idea of day-off casual wear. A cap with TriCounty Financial on it. A thick watch. He gripped the rail at the end of the bed like he was gripping the back of a chair at a meeting, lording over the other agents. "They say things are going to get better for you. All signs pointing skyward. And the prosthetics these days, seriously, you'll run faster now than you did at Quantico."

Stoudemire gave Rome's left and only foot a shake.

"And don't worry. Government health care, it's the best. You won't have to worry about a thing. They'll even fix your cabin up so you can get around easier. Widen the doors, install bars, ramps, toilet."

If he could have gotten out of bed right then. If he could've strangled his good buddy Shane Stoudemire.

"I was sorry to hear about Wyatt. Good man. I talked to his brother yesterday. Good man. Sounded like you two were off on some kind of adventure."

Did Rome's eyes get wider? Could he stop them from doing so? Could he try?

"Fishing? On the Gulf? Swordfish?"

Rome blinked. Tried to nod.

"You know, as soon as they found what was in Wyatt's carry-on, we got a call. The photos, the rumors, all of it. And it made its way to me pretty fast. I still have an alert on Lafitte if anything comes in over the transom, mainly to make sure you're staying out of it. But you were never going to stay out of it, no matter how much we told you to leave it alone. I get it. I really do."

*No you don't, and you never will, you condescending—*

"I really hope they're wrong. I hope you're not so brain-damaged you don't register what I'm saying. I hope every word is loud and clear deep inside, brother."

"Mmnuu." No, not now. Not like that.

"Very good, very good." A pat on the leg. *The* leg. "So which one was Batman, and which one was Robin? Look, I get it. I wish this was easier. But Lafitte's really good. Really good. And you are not."

Rome breathed heavier, and he couldn't help if it came out as pants and grunts. Fucking awful. Fucking ridiculous.

"You are a failure, a burnout, a drunk, and a suicide

risk. Now you can't even kill yourself. So listen, something for you to chew on." He pulled the chair over and sat real close to Rome's head, leaned in. "Yes, somebody found him. And he showed up again on the Gulf Coast a fucking month ago, and caused more damage in one or two days than most hurricanes cause. The only reason you didn't hear about it was because we kept the lid on. You've been drooling all over yourself for *a month*, man."

Rome closed his eyes. It was one of the very few things he had control of on his body. They'd already caught the bastard. What was Stoudemire leading up to?

The douche kept going. "He killed a teenager first thing in the morning, injured another one badly. They didn't know who they were fucking with. He was sleeping in a truck full of vitamins, protein shake mixes, and a shit-ton of anabolic steroids, so there's that. Then he stole a car, stole some motorcycles, crashed the motorcycles, but he was just getting started."

Rome remembered trying to lure Lafitte down South when he had disappeared the first time, joined up with those bikers. Instead, he ended up having to fly to Sioux Falls because the whole thing was a major fuck up. His wife followed him on a separate flight, and they had a short reunion before she took things into her own hands. She was going to kill Lafitte herself in a hotel stairwell. He got her first.

Stoudemire: "You know Ginny Lafitte, right? And by the way, I always assumed you fucked her. Did you fuck her, Franklin? No comment? Okay."

Jesus, that poor...already half-crazy by the time Rome met her, hoping she could help get Billy to come home.

Bait on a rat trap. But it turned out the motherfucker had done more of a number on Ginny's head than anyone realized. Some serious mental gymnastics. Girl went and tried to kill herself. And from what he'd heard, she never stopped trying after.

Stoudemire raised his fingers to his lip like a Japanese schoolgirl. "Oh my, you noticed my faux pas? I said *knew*, as in past tense, as in—"

"*Muuah-thuk—*"

"Almost dead. They saved her, but she's a vegetable. Big ol' potato now. Lafitte wrapped a leather belt around her neck and hung her on a coat hook behind the door of her hospital room. Just. Like. That."

The douche scrunched his eyebrows and then reached for a tissue off the bedside table. "Hold up, looks like a bit of a nosebleed. Let me get it for you."

Rome fought a little, but couldn't move very well. Stoudemire rubbed the tissue under his nose, and then pinched his nostrils closed for a sec, pulled the tissue away. Sure enough, it was soaked in red. Rome tasted pennies in his mouth and tried to swallow. He choked, started coughing. Stoudemire was all "Whoa, buddy, let me get the nurse." He punched the button, but someone must have already heard, because two of those damned nursing assistants came in, one girl, one boy, all smiles, pulling on latex gloves. Stoudemire backed away while they lifted Rome's bed, pulled him forward and pounded on his back, offered him some water, still not asking him what happened. Not like he could answer, but still.

While they were pounding, Stoudemire stood near the door, his concerned look so fucking phony. He patiently waited to give Rome more details. Fuck his superior bullshit. Rome started pointing at Stoudemire, *Get him out! Get him out!*

They understood, the little nursettes. They sure the hell did. So they shuffled Stoudemire out of the room while the male nursette kept patting Rome's back.

One thought: Billy Lafitte might be a murderous, traitorous blob of cunt pus, but he would never kill Ginny.

Then he realized what Stoudemire *hadn't* told him. It would've been the first thing. They still hadn't caught Billy. He had escaped again.

Bad news, good news.

# CHAPTER NINETEEN

Manuel said he had to go out, asked Billy if he wanted anything.

Lafitte reminded him about the nitro. "Can't you buy it over the counter?"

"Not how it works, boyo. Not how it works."

"Do you know anybody? Some friends or something? Don't they always have extra lying around?"

Manuel shrugged and said he would check.

After eating another slice of the pizza, Lafitte drank a few short glasses of water and then wandered into the real living room, the one with the old-fashioned cabinet TV and lived-in furniture and cat toys and old carpet. Wood panels. Those took real commitment these days.

In the corner, a small bookcase-type box, kind of. Three shelves, a stack of newspapers and photo albums on the bottom, a couple of framed photos in the middle, and on top, a laminated poster curled at the corners, a painting of a skull-faced woman. A skull painted on her face, a sugar skull. The poster had been stapled to the bookcase. In front of her, a statue of a grim reaper, scythe in hand, except in a much more bedazzled gown, holding a crystal ball.

Scattered at the feet of the reaper, several photos. Headshots, like they had been cut from school pictures or from driver's licenses. All men, most young, most Hispanic, and then...an old DL photo of Billy Lafitte.

Mid-twenties, he would guess by the hair, high and tight, before he got into the Gene Vincent thing. Some sort of potpourri sprinkled on top, too. And then, the candles. Those glass Mexican Catholic things he'd seen in truck stops and drug stores. First, a blue candle with yellow art, Saint Dymphna. Never heard of her. The second looked to be a hand-drawn Sacred Heart of Jesus, white art, red candle. The last one, one he'd heard of but never seen. Very simple, a white candle, black art. Another reaper, crude, holding a skull. In bold on top, **LA SANTISIMA MUERTE**, and on the bottom, **HOLY DEATH**.

Lafitte picked it up. It had been burned lately. About a third of it gone. Supposed to be some cult-like figure, the Saint of Death, but she was a big deal, especially with the narcos and their families. She could protect them here, above ground, or she could protect them in the land of the dead after they bit it.

Or, he guessed, you didn't need to be a narco to be under her protection.

He heard Jimena's shuffle behind him, a tittering *no no no no no* until she was right there, yanking the candle from his hand and bowing to it, putting it back, saying, "Don't touch! Don't touch! Say you're sorry and don't touch! Did you touch anything else? Did you?"

He shook his head. A little stunned. He'd never thought her to be superstitious, and only a little religious. Maybe "cover your bets" religious.

"It's bad luck. But you'll probably be okay, since, you know."

He pointed to his photo. "That's me?"

Jimena shrugged. "You left some stuff at your old

place. They called and asked us if we wanted it, since you were already gone. Manuel brought it home."

"What else?"

"Photos, you and your mother and cousins, and, well, and Ginny."

"And Ham?"

She raised her eyes and made the sign of the cross. "So sad, so sad, when did I see him last? Was he barely walking? Did he barely have hair?"

"And Savannah?"

Jimena gathered both of his hands in hers. Squeezed. "You know she will come looking for you one day. When her grandparents have long lost influence. She will come for you then."

He wanted to pull his hands away but didn't dare. Not from witchy woman, no, he didn't dare. "If you say so. Cast a spell."

"No, not...no spells." She let go, waved her hand over the shrine. "Simply prayer. Some people need more help than others."

"Like me?"

"You, my cousins, see? And him, he's my uncle, but that's an old picture. He died long before. Now, we pray Santa Muerte watches over him."

He didn't ask the obvious: *in Hell? Hell?* Why the hell else would he need a prayer once he was already in Hell? Jesus, in Hell. C'mon. People in Heaven don't need the living praying for them. Instead, Lafitte pointed to the Dymphna candle. "Who's she?"

"For the voices. You know? The demon voices, they speak to you and no one else can hear? You pray to her to help soothe the voices."

"Does it help?"

"With the right medicine. Anyway, don't worry about it. You should feel it. Whatever you do, wherever you go, know the Saints are watching out for you. Okay? We pray for you. We pray you win all the time."

"I didn't, I didn't realize you were like this. Narco?"

She shook her head, smiled. "My cousins. My uncle."

"And me?"

"Manuel's idea. It took me a few days to notice he had added your photo to the altar."

Lafitte nodded. "Cool."

Jimena bent down and picked up a box of tall matches, flicked one alight and lit each candle in turn, saving Santa Muerte for last. The prayer under her breath, all Spanish, hurried and rhythmic.

The voices. Maybe that's why she talked so much. To drown out those voices.

# CHAPTER TWENTY

Lo-Wider's grampa's Monte Carlo wouldn't be released from impound for a while, and it was all coming out of his hide or his pocket, or both, already the old man's rasp getting in his head. But since he didn't have wheels, DeVaughn handed over a Discover card and told him to go rent what he needed, make it a week. Seriously. So he went down to the rental place and got himself a Nissan Armada. Big ass SUV, got the satellite radio built-in and wi-fi and all that shit. Leather seats. If it was his, he'd have some upgrades to do—front grill, rims, more speakers—but as a rental, it was better than he could've hoped. He *fit* in it. The cockpit had plenty of room. His ass didn't slough off the seat. He could even wear the seatbelt, if he wanted to.

YP was along with him. Seemed a smart enough guy, maybe a bit cocky. Bit cocky and thin, too. Arms like rope. Neck like rope. Legs like...all of him looked like rope. Hard-twisted, burnt-on-both-ends rope. Even wore his clothes tighter than the usual BGM so girls could notice his muscles. Muscles was all he had to show. Brains didn't show.

Lo-Wider spun down the volume on Waka Flocka Flame, "Round of Applause", as they turned onto the right street. Blue collar, shit. This was *no* collar. This was spic territory. Neither would admit it, but they got nervous, they sure did, because spics just *kill* your ass.

No posturing. No playing. They cut you and then get other spics to write a song about it.

In the meantime, this song—*Bus' it, bus' it, bus' it...*

One thing Lo-Wider never expected was getting sent to do some espionage. Some *RE-con.* All he'd wanted was some money, get himself known to DeVaughn so maybe he could learn some things about poker. Face it, Lo-Wider was never going to get fit, never going to get those six-pack abs. So what he wanted was to do what DeVaughn did.

Not what YP was itching to do.

"That one?" The little banger thumbed the house.

"Mm-hm."

Cute little flowerbed. Garage, but a car outside. These people, the spics, used the garage as an extra room, cramming so many into one house—wait, who was Lo-Wider to judge when he knew damn well he was living with grampa, grampa's girlfriend, Aunt Eve, Uncle Gummy, two girl cousins and three boy cousins? Shit. Sorry, spics.

"Alright, let's do this." YP reached for the door handle.

"What? What are we going to do?"

"Why do you think we're here?"

"To wait and see if we see Lafitte."

"So I'm going to go see if I see him."

Lo-Wider let out a breath and said, "No, no, listen, we watch from the street. If we get caught—"

"—we get caught, we invade this motherfucker. Pow! Pow! Motherfuckers be dead. Like the man said."

Holy shit, the itty-bity psychopath. "Uhn-uh, no, you crazy! DeVaughn wants this one. This here, it's personal.

That cop shot his brother, you know."

YP looked, like, disgusted. "I ain't no errand boy. No one told me shit."

"What, you thought we were going to strap up and go in two-fisted?"

"I only go in two-fisted on your mama."

"What?"

"You heard me."

He climbed out of the Armada and started across the street, through the yard and over the side-gate into the backyard. Lo-Wider struggled to free himself from the cockpit. Even if it was roomier, it was still a tight fit when it came to twisting himself sideways and trying to get out without pulling some muscles. By the time he was out, trying to close the door gently, YP was already out of sight. Lo-Wider's insides tightened up, like, same as when he ate Qdoba burritos. Something about the beans. Barely got the last bite down before he had to find a stall.

He sure as hell wasn't going to follow YP around the house. Maybe it would be okay. Maybe YP was all mouth. Sure seemed it. Smart enough except when it was time to shut up. Should Lo-Wider call DeVaughn? Tell him about another fuck-up today? He was trying to get on the nigga's good side. Might start by not calling him nigga. Mr. DeVaughn. Mr. Rose. Brother DeVaughn?

No, he wasn't going to bring the bad news. He was going to wait it out. Lean against his new Armada and wait it out. YP was all mouth. He wasn't even packing. Lo-Wider was sure of it. Jesus, hot out here, going on seven o'clock at night. His clothes were already sour with sweat from the rest of the day—wet, dry, wet, dry, wet again. He'd rather be inside playing penny ante online, trying to win a few tickets into tournaments. He was too shy to try it on the boats yet, which is why he needed lessons from Mr. DeVaughn. But he wasn't that bad. Problem was these fuckers didn't play the way they were supposed to play online for pennies. They did crazy shit. How was he supposed to know if it was a bluff? How was he supposed to guess with a real face to look at? Those motherfuckers might go down hard, but they ended up taking half the table with them.

He thought about his game a few nights back. There was no way he would've folded three-of-a-kind except this kid with twice as many pennies kept pushing the bet higher and higher, and, goddamn it. Lo-Wider folded. He never knew what the other player, handled TikTok with a hoodie and sunglasses icon photo, really had. He should've called. He would never be like DeVaughn until he—

That scream, tho. Piercing. A woman. Oh Jesus. Oh Jesus.


Didn't matter what the fat motherfucker had to say. Like he was in charge? Like he was going to be the one lay down the law? Fuck Lo-Wider. And fuck DeVaughn Rose. The Mob was doing DeVaughn a favor, not the other way around. A BGM kills Lafitte, that's some righteous shit. Put DeVaughn in his place. Old man. Couldn't clean up his own trash.

So YP climbed out of the Armada—seriously? Could've had an Escalade. Could've had a Lexus. Motherfucker picked a *Nissan?*—and was going to do some damage to somebody somehow. Didn't matter if Lafitte was here or not. They knew this was his people's house. Step-people, anyway. Hurting them meant hurting Lafitte. It went without saying. Unless Lafitte already did them himself. I mean, motherfucker already killed his own *wife* today. But seriously, she was a crazy bitch, what YP heard, so she didn't count. Crazy bitch wife ain't the same as your people, even your step-people.

YP took a peek for dogs through the slats. Some neighbor dogs yapping, sure, growling, but not in the backyard he was about to go in. Call it luck, call it God. Call it something. The gate was locked. Okay. Pulled himself up, pulled himself over, easy. Nothing much back here. Deck furniture, Weber grill. Few pots with tomato plants, hot peppers. YP took out his blade. Badass. Folding knife, black, titanium, stumpy but serrated. He'd done some damage to motherfuckers with his little blade. Or one motherfucker, and then this dog had barked at him, someone's pit. Fuck that. One less pitbull in the world, he did that bit-to-shit hound a favor.

Flat against the back wall of the house. First window he came to, sneaked a look. Right? It was what he expected—garage was half boxes, half some sort of guest room. He moved on. Next window. Kitchen. Empty, but a little TV was on. A sliding glass door was next, also into the kitchen. He tried the handle and it slid right open. Made a bad screeching noise, so he slowed it down, eased it along at glacier speed. Felt like it, but glaciers, man, that was some real slow shit right there. Glaciers could pulverize mammoths, houses, all kinds of shit. And they were melting, which would fuck things up even more. He should name his blade "Glacier." And he should keep it in the freezer until he was ready to use it.

The thing about YP, he was book smart. He liked science. He liked history. But, goddamn, he didn't like the other kids who liked that shit. So he played his part. Loyal banger, even if he was taking classes at the community college in secret. A couple at a time, paying cash. As far as his mom knew, it was scholarship. Smart wasn't the problem at all. Being dissed for being smart was the problem.

YP. "Young Psychopath." Bored and brilliant. Bad combo. He liked to hurt people. He liked to show he was smarter than them. He knew how to hide in plain sight and play white people games and also hide in baggy jeans and boxers and play black people games. Two lives. Like Batman.

Inside the kitchen, he didn't bother closing the glass door. The cold air from the house rushed out the back and vaporized and left YP feeling clammy. But he hardened himself to the fear and nausea and kept on. He was hunting. It was a motherfucking rush. Let the fat fucker outside do it DeVaughn's way. Black man seeking revenge shouldn't be wearing a fine suit like DeVaughn's if he was afraid to get it dirty. Should only be wearing a suit like DeVaughn's if he played for the NFL or if he preached in church. YP would carve up this Lafitte and send DeVaughn some pics from his phone. Dead dead dead. Now pay up and go back to your card games.

Poker bored YP. Too easy.

The house was quiet. There was a TV on the counter on, but muted. And wouldn't you know it, there was some breaking news: a plane crash on one side of the screen, and a reporter on the other standing outside a hospital, it looked like, in Mobile. Big news day. He walked lightly. He had spent hours and hours walking around at night at home, learning how to make himself a ninja in Jordans. How to anticipate creaking boards, squeaky shoes, sticky linoleum. Took weeks and weeks, but he got to the point he could get the tip of his blade a millimeter from the eye of whatever piece of shit was passed out in his mother's bed without them ever knowing. If he had wanted to, he could've snuffed out every one of them useless, leaching bullshit wannabes. It was only his mother's happiness kept him from doing so. Maybe it was the wrong way to be happy, getting used and abused the way she did. But everyone had a different happy, and he'd learned this was hers. But it still made him feel good to know that if he wanted to, lights out.

"The Glacier" in the eye, and that was that.

Lots of framed photos on the walls of the hallways. Spic family portraits, but mostly a small woman with flyaway hair and wild eyes, and a dark-toned man with a slick pomp and a heavy mustache. Tired eyes. Looked thirty years out of style. Then the den. Dark except for some candles burning in the far corner. Those Saint candles. And skulls and shit. Voodoo.

Bullshit, all of it. YP knew better. He was all about reason. He was an atheist. As long as his mom and his friends didn't know, he was cool. Made it a lot easier to explain why he was wired the way he was. Same with other psychopaths. He'd read tons about them, the serial killers, the dictators, the cult leaders. YP made more sense when he put himself among their ranks.

Some chirping, chattering, coming from the next

hallway. Was it a bird? Canary? He thought it might be. No, no, it was a person. A whistle here and there, a little sing-song. But in-between were words. Not English. Spanish. He knew a little Spanish. Had to if you were dealing with drugs. Had to go to the source for better prices, so he'd learned enough to do deals. Nothing this voice said, high and chirpy, made much sense. Things like, "My grandson, I never knew you," and "Sweet boy, may the Holy Death guide your father back to you one day," and even some singing, like, "We drank a toast to innocence, we drank a toast to time." A slight echo, her voice bouncing off tile.

Yeah, no bird. It was the crazy-haired lady from the photos. Another step farther along. The bathroom door was not closed all the way, a line of light glowing from it.

One, two, three.

He kicked the door wide open and moved fast. Blade up. The woman was on the toilet, shorts and panties on the ground. She dropped the phone she was texting on. Looked at him with wide-open crazy eyes and let out a scream.

YP smiled. "Bitch! I ain't give you a reason to scream yet!"


Lo-Wider ran toward the scream. He hated running, goddamn it, but he had to get in there and stop YP from fucking this up any more. He'd known there was something about him. How he had this look, like he was always better than everybody else. Smarter.

But meaner, too.

Fuck trying to jump the fence. Why not try the front door? So he tried it. Locked. He pounded on it. "Yo, P. C'mon man. C'mon. We've got to book it." Pound some more. "Let me *in*, nigga! You hearin' me?"

The dogs around the neighborhood were going nuts. Even one inside the house right here, barking at him pounding on the door. Lo-Wider was a big boy, right? He could bust this thing down. So Lo-Wider stepped back and took a hard look at the door. Took a run at it and slammed his shoulder into it. It was a bowling ball on a waterbed. Fucking ball didn't feel a thing. The waterbed, though—

"Fuck!" He held his shoulder. He seethed a little before going back to the door, trying the knob again, a hard twist, while pushing all he had against it. Hard, man, hard! Hold your breath! Nothing. He pounded again. "C'mon, man!"

Lady was still screaming.

"Come on! Let! Me! In!"

The door swung open while he was still attached to it, and he almost fell into the front hallway and on the angry little dog, barking and growling. Only thing keeping him up was sheer will because it was this Lafitte motherfucker, the same one who'd killed Bossman and Isiah, same one who'd stolen his grampa's Monte Carlo, who opened the door. All cleaned up, but still, yeah, still him. Lafitte held up a finger. "You! You stay here!"

And he headed off down the hall toward the screaming, little dog right behind him.

His guts pained some more, but Lo-Wider got over it and stepped into the house, knowing there were others now watching from their front yards and the street.

Disaster. Why was he even bothering to stick around? Go ahead, leave YP to his fate, thinks he's so smart.

But no, running away wasn't the BGM thing to do. Couldn't leave a soldier behind. Even though he wasn't BGM, he didn't want them so pissed that he got blacklisted. He leaned up against the wall in the front hallway and caught his breath. Hearing the woman shouting, "He's got a knife! Be careful!" and YP shouting, "Mother*fucker* let me go mother*fucker!*" and the dog still, "*GrrrrrARK grrrrrARK!*" and not a word from Lafitte. A whole lot of slamming into walls and banging and shaking.

Even with shin splints, Lo-Wider kept on going, letting the wall hold him up, flinching when it boomed again and the picture frames rattled. He stepped down into the den, dark except for candles in the corner and the light coming from the next hallway. Lafitte banged backwards against the wall outside the bathroom. He had YP's arms locked up above him, the little knife tight in his fist. YP kicked at the doorframe, kept slamming Lafitte into the wall, but Lafitte wasn't letting go. The little dog danced around and nipped at YP while he kicked the doorframe and pushed and then kicked the dog and then tried to turn his head to bite Lafitte's arm but nothing was working.

Lafitte saw Lo-Wider standing there, shouted, "Stay the fuck back! I told you to stay put!"

YP all like, "Motherfucker, get this motherfucker off of me!"

Lo-Wider looked around. He wasn't about to let Lafitte get a hand on him. He saw what had happened to Isiah, tough nigga, and Bossman, tough white boy.

Twigs, man. Like motherfucking twigs. Looked around, needed something heavy. Like, what, one of those framed photos on the wall? Too light. How about the TV? Too big. Shit, where was a baseball bat or a golf club or a fucking shotgun when you needed one?

The candles, though.

He ran to the corner and grabbed one of the glass Catholic candles, a long wick and big flame, and ran over to the fight and waited until YP kicked the doorframe again, pushing him and Lafitte toward the living room, back first, and a little spic lady escaped the bathroom and ran the other way, and Lo-Wider started banging the fucking candle on Lafitte's head over and over until the fucker smashed into pieces and cut Lo-Wider and burned his hand a little and—

*Whoosh*

—Lafitte's head went up in flames like a barbecue. Holy shit! Like Michael Jackson back in the day. Lafitte let go of YP real fast and starting screaming and trying to bat out his hair fire with his hands, turning in circles, all over the den, some flames slinging off and starting smaller fires. Screams. Bad screams. Lo-Wider looked at his bloody hand with shards of glass and some blisters coming up and, shit, it really hurt, but holy shit—

YP got himself together and was all smiles. Gave his arms a couple of spins in the air to loosen up, twisted his neck, and then took two big steps toward the screaming Lafitte and planted his stubby blade into the man's tricep and *twist* and out and into his shoulder and *twist* and out and aiming for his neck but got his arm again and *twist* and—

The pops weren't loud. Lafitte screamed louder. But

there were a lot of them. YP looked all confused for a few seconds. Left his knife in Lafitte and turned left and right, slapping at himself. But it was the old woman from the bathroom, advancing toward him, arm straight out with a pistol popping off shots. Lo-Wider figured it out, a twenty-two, the last couple in YP's face before he went down. By then Lafitte was on the floor, the old lady rushed over, trying to put out the fire with her T-shirt, and the other fires in the room were spreading fast. Everywhere Lafitte slung his head, new fires popped off, some rising fast up the wood panel walls.

Once she'd put out Lafitte's head, the woman swung around, gun out at Lo-Wider, and fired off a couple of shots before he could get his hands up, and *bam* in the belly and *bam* in the ear and it didn't hurt for a good ten seconds or so. It was...pressure. The sort of pressure that made you tighten your gut and grunt and think if you ever let go again, you was going to die. But when the pain started, it *fucking started*, and he wailed, oh, did he ever wail.

Not only because he was bad hurt, but also because there was the grim reaper standing in the corner, sur-rounded by hellfire.

# CHAPTER TWENTY-ONE

The smell of burnt hair and pomade made Lafitte's throat tighten up. Coughed. The skin on his scalp rose, blistered, same on the back of his neck, and a long stripe across his face, over his eye, nose, cheek. Jimena had gotten the fire out, but the damage had already begun creeping out to every patch of fried skin, pulsing the pain signals bad, man, so bad, and Lafitte knew he had to get up and go before it incapacitated him. He would heal, again. He would be ugly for a while and it would hurt like shit and steal his sleep, but he would heal. It wasn't important right now.

He blinked. A blistered eyelid, man. Jimena brushed the glass from his hair and shoulders. Then he noticed the fires, how the flames were tickling the fingers of the dead banger on the floor beside him. It was freaky watching a body get taken by fire, just lying there and taking it when you expect anything human-shaped to jump up and run the fuck away.

"Out, Jimena, we've got to get out."

"Look at you! Oh, Billy, look at what they've done to you!"

"Outside!" He gave her a push and felt a sting. His palms, blisters popped, now wet, the skin coming off in rolls. Shit, when he'd grabbed his hair, shit, his hands. Shit. He looked around, but the fire was growing and he was one big wick and there was no time. He saw the fat kid rolling on the floor, a couple of gunshot wounds, one in his gut and one that had made his ear a mess. Those damned twenty-twos. Took six or seven and a lucky close-up to the face to kill the one with the blade.

He grabbed the back of the fat kid's shirt. "Get up, goddamn it."

Fat kid fanned his hand at the side of his head. "She shot me! I'm shot! I'm fucking dying!"

"Get up! Get up or I'll kill you!"

"I can't...I can't...I can't..."

Lafitte kicked him on the leg. He screeched real bad. Lafitte grabbed him under the arm. "Get the fuck up." Couldn't lift him, but he kept the pressure on. Tried to keep the skin on his hands from shredding more, but goddamn, what was he supposed to do?

Kid finally got up and looked back over his shoulder. "YP? You hear me, man?"

"Guy's dead. Get out of here!" Hand on his shirt again, not going to let this one run far. He was the path to DeVaughn. The yellow-brick road. They both made it out front, where the whole yard was filled with neighbors and kids and people holding up their phones to make this shit go viral, which was the last thing Lafitte needed. Nothing he could do.

He let go of the fat kid's shirt, and he dropped onto the grass and rolled around, starting up with the fanning again, crying, "Shit, Jesus, shit, Jesus, shit, help me Jesus!"

Lafitte found Jimena on her knees in the yard, her shirt and hands stained black with ash, but otherwise alright, jabbering to another Spanish-speaking neighbor who was standing over her shoulder.

Manuel wasn't back yet, still no nitro. Lafitte had run out of time. He needed to get out of here now, and this fat kid was going along. But Lafitte finally got a good look at his palms, scalded through and through. But he felt...numb. Going into shock.

Fuck shock. Shock was for later. Shock was for people who could afford it.

Friendly neighbors were starting to pay attention to him now. Asking if he needed an ambulance or a towel or, Jesus, *Are you okay are you okay are you okay?*

"Fuck no, I'm not okay! Can't you see I'm not fucking okay?"

All of them stared at his face, his scalp, his hands. "Oh. My. God."

"Get me some duct tape. Right now. I need some duct tape."

One of the neighbors threw a beach towel over Lafitte's shoulder but was too freaked to throw it across both shoulders, so he caught it in his hand before it fell to the ground. Felt like grabbing a handful of rusty steel wool. Peeling it off was worse. Sirens coming. There were always sirens coming. He couldn't get through a full day anymore without sirens coming, let alone today when it was every hour, it seemed. More sirens. Who were they this time? Cops first? Firetrucks? Ambulance?

Ambulance.

He glanced over at Jimena, standing among her friends now, wild gestures with her hands, telling the story. Leaving out Lafitte, he hoped. Maybe he was a visiting cousin. She would tell them something believable. But the authorities would know. They would figure it out and give her and Manuel a hard time, goddamn it.

More of Lafitte's bizarro King Midas touch.

"Here!"

One of the neighbors was back with a half-used roll of duct tape. Big, thick, silver duct tape. Lafitte grabbed it and started at his wrist and taped one of his hands, one two three wraps, leaving his fingers and thumb free. They'd gotten skinned too, but not as bad. He still needed them. He flexed the silver hand. Hurt like all holy fuck, but he could deal. He started to wrap the other one when someone reached out and grabbed his arm.

"Help's on the way! You don't have to!"

Lafitte kept wrapping. "They can't help me. Thanks, though."

He held onto the duct tape, but then, pain coming back to him, remembered there was a fucking knife in his back. He handed the tape to the well-wisher. "See the knife? Pull it out. Slap some tape on it."

"But help's coming, it's almost here, it'll be here in a minute."

He held up the roll of tape. "Anybody?"

One of the slack-jawed teenagers standing around, shirtless, skateboard on the ground beside him, stepped up. "Yeah, cool."

Kid got the knife out and the tape patch on, said it was still bleeding.

"Fuck! More tape! Wrap the shoulder!"

Wrapped the shoulder, another neighbor helping now. Then around the upper arm to plug another hole. It felt awful, but the guys made sure the tape was tight and nothing was leaking. Good ol' duct tape.

He broke through the crowd as the first fire truck

showed up alongside a cop cruiser. For once, he was glad of the crowd. Good cover. The smoke had finally started pouring out the front door and through the roof, and even more people cramped themselves into the yard to watch as the cops shouted for everyone to "Get back! Across the street, now!" One of them called for back-up. An ambulance showed up. The road was getting thick with whirling lights and big machines.

Lafitte found the fat kid on the lawn where he'd left him, on his hands and knees now, trying to puke but not getting anywhere with it. A long string of spit and some dry hacks. Lafitte walked over and nudged him with his boot. "Let's go."

"Told you...told you I was *dying* here, man." Fat kid was going to hyperventilate. "I need help! I need help now! I need my grampa. Get my grampa over here!"

Another nudge, harder. Lafitte scooped under his arm, not caring if the kid wanted to move or not. "We ain't got time. You want to talk to cops or talk to DeVaughn?"

"Serious?"

"Cops? DeVaughn? You know where DeVaughn is?"

"I want...I want...I want a doctor, man."

Lafitte knelt beside him. Hissed, "Cops'll give you a doctor. After they're done with you, I mean. Hey, look at this."

The kid turned his head. Lafitte lifted the little knife, set the edge of it on the kid's shredded ear. "Your friend left this in my shoulder. How about I finish off your ear there?"

"No, man! Please!"

"Get your ass up and get us the fuck out of here."

Kid was slow, but he did as he was told.

"Good, good," Lafitte said, loud enough to be heard. "We're going to get you some help."

Slung the kid's elephant-leg-of-an-arm over his head—*Damn!*—and said, "Which one's yours?"

"Got the…got the…the…"

They passed a cop, who asked if they needed help. Lafitte chinned toward the ambulance. "Heading over now."

"Let me help?"

"I got it. You want to help Jimena? See her over there? She's my aunt. She's got some burns."

"So do you! Jesus, fuck, man!"

"I'll live."

Young white cop sure enough didn't want to carry around a freak like Lafitte and this fat ass black kid. Could see it in his eyes. "Okay, we'll get your aunt some help, buddy."

Fat kid finally got out, "It's the Nissan? The big SUV?"

Lafitte held up his keys, punched the fob. The lights flickered and the doors clicked. They headed for it. A few feet, then a few inches, then Lafitte opened the back passenger door and told the fat kid, "Climb in."

Took him a huge fucking effort. Now it got a different cop's attention. He came over and said, "You can't leave."

"He's got to go to the hospital!"

"Calm down, there's EMTs right over there."

"We don't have time to wait, he got his ear burned off!"

"Hold up!" He turned and shouted to an EMT. Then

back. "Hold up. We'll get him there. Let this guy work on him first. No need to panic."

The cop was older, in his forties, and Lafitte realized he knew the prick. His name tag, SPIVELY, and as quick is it clicked into Lafitte's mind, it must have clicked in Spively's, too, because his eyes went wide and his hand went for his pistol. Not even for the tazer or the pepper spray. Right for the gun. Lafitte got there right as Spively wrapped his hand over the grip. Lafitte held the man's hand and his gun down down down, hard, gonna keep his gun in the holster and fuck you fuck you fuck you—

Lafitte said, "We really going to do this now?"

"Billy Lafitte, you are under arrest." Straining. "You have...no*where*...to...*go*."

"No, not you. You don't get to bring me down."

"Quit...*resisting*." Louder.

Shit.

Lafitte headbutted the fuck out of the cop. He went limp. Lafitte reached around, held him up with one arm while prying the gun from his hand and holster with the other. He wasn't out, stunned, same as Lafitte's skull, too, but he gave Spively another loud *crack* to the forehead before dropping him, slamming the door, and running around to the driver's side. Stumbling. Holding himself up, leaning against the SUV. Once inside, he grabbed the key from the fat kid and saw flashing blues and greens pulsing in and out of focus as he tried to find the ignition. Easier once he heard the gunshots. Saw the cops surrounding the Armada, pistols out.

Key, in. Crank. Go go go go!

Swerved around the fire truck directly ahead, two cruisers behind it, then up into someone's yard. Fuck the street. He went right through a chainlink fence into a backyard, swerved again to avoid a swingset, an inflatable pool, an old man mowing his lawn. Through another chainlink fence. The next fence was plastic. Dogs, pretty sure he hit a dog. Shit, where was Kaiser? Jimena would keep him. Jimena would help him get home. Out the front gate and back on the road, and he needed to get himself gone fast.

Lafitte shouted into the back seat, "Where we going?"

"Oh Jesus oh God oh Grampa oh fuck oh fuck—"

"Focus, champ! DeVaughn! Where is DeVaughn?"

"I don't know! I don't know!"

"Where's your phone? Call him! Call him!"

"I lost my phone! Oh Jesus! I need my grampa, man! Take me home!"

"You get your grampa when I get DeVaughn!"

"Please!"

"Fuck please! DeVaughn!"

"Okay, okay, okay, I'll call him, find me a phone, I call him, oh God it hurts it hurts so bad, man!"

The fat kid was all he had. Goddamn it. Worthless. He brushed his hand through his hair and forgot he had taped his hand and that his scalp was all crispy hair and blistered skin, felt the blisters breaking as the tape scraped across. Made him shiver all over. The shock, he couldn't run from it for too much longer. His chest felt as if the fat kid was sitting on it. He had needed a couple days, that was all, a couple days to get his wind back, but he had gotten less than seven hours instead.

Getting dark. Sunset over the Gulf of Mexico. Maybe his last one, right? The way things were going...

Why not end it the same way Ginny did? Walk out

into the Gulf and keep going, let it wash over him. That would be dignifying. The sharks might have at his body, the forces of nature might fuck up what was left royally before he washed back ashore, but he wouldn't have known it. Some poor fucking cop would be responsible for cleaning up the mess. Some weak-stomached patrol officer would discover pieces of Lafitte and projectile vomit into the sand. Lafitte would be the dignified one. He would take a big drink of seawater and lose consciousness and the last thing he would hear is water.

He should have known the angel on his shoulder would get outvoted by the devil, who told him: *Not until DeVaughn is dead.*

Lafitte sighed. It hurt to sigh. The devil was right, even if Lafitte didn't want him to be.

"Five minutes," he told the fat kid. "You're going to be alright, buddy."

Highway 90. Beachfront. A beautiful summer evening. A wailing kid missing an ear in the backseat.

Better a missing ear than a missing head. He'd seen worse.

# CHAPTER TWENTY-TWO

The call from Lo-Wider was all wrong and the kid was smart enough to realize DeVaughn would know it, too. The tone, the pitch, the words themselves. Too formal. Too...something. A weird feeling.

DeVaughn told him where they could meet in Gulfport, the parking garage of the casino hotel. He hung up and thought about how to prepare. Either Lafitte had Lo-Wider as a hostage, or had flipped him over to his side. Didn't matter. This thing was going to happen now, and DeVaughn wasn't going to do the James Bond villain shit of talking so much that Bond escapes and murders his ass. They made fun of it so much, who was it, Austin Powers? And still, mother-fuckers always got to toy with James Bond instead of just shoot his ass.

Not this time. Billy Lafitte ain't no motherfucking James Bond. Never was, never will be.

They sat in the parking garage, in the new Lincoln MKZ they'd picked up at a rental joint. White one. All the extras. Still no connection between them and the dealership in Mobile, so as far as the rental place was concerned, they would get the car back in about five days, as soon as DeVaughn and Melissa "flew back home" from their vacation.

DeVaughn grinned thinking about it. The rental joint would never see this car again. DeVaughn wouldn't be flying anywhere anytime soon. Melissa, god only knew what would happen to her. Prison? Or would she call the whole thing a kidnapping, big nigger forced me? That was okay, too. Whatever she had to do, he'd back her up. Whatever it took to keep her free. She was worth it. This whole day, if it ended with Lafitte dead and DeVaughn in true love with Melissa, will have been worth it.

He looked over at Melissa, one leg propped on the dash, the other stretched on the floorboard. Her seat was reclined some. She held her arms over her head, a yawn and a stretch. She caught him looking and smiled. Beamed.

She said, "Can I come out and say it? You don't have to say it back or get all weird."

"What?"

"Like, you don't have to treat me any differently, or think I'm expecting something."

"Girl, I love you, too. How's that?"

She rolled her eyes. "Oh, great, now you're going to be all up on my jock all the time? I can't be tied down."

"But baby, baby please—"

Hand in his face. "Uhn-uh. You need to be there when I give you a call, but that's the extent of it."

They both cracked up. DeVaughn tried one more, "I promise, baby, I'll be good."

Melissa threw her head back and it was a full-on cackle. This was fun. When was the last time he'd been with someone and it was fun this way? He shook his head. "Can you tell me what's going on with us?"

"Well, didn't you say so? I was going to say, too. I love you. I mean it. I love you."

"Yeah, I know, right? But it's only been a day. One day. Have you ever…you know, seriously, not a little somethin' somethin', but real full-on love?"

Melissa shrugged. "Maybe once or twice. But it wasn't like he felt the same way. This time, you do."

"So what is it? What's going on? Are we crazy?"

She moved closer, head on his shoulder. "I remember this guy, a youth pastor or something, telling me love is a verb. It's something you do. People try to think about it too much, you can think yourself out of it because the devil or the world makes you selfish. But love is something, when you do it, you want to keep doing it. It's a muscle."

"I can dig it."

"Really? You can 'dig' it? How old are you?"

"Quit it, bitch, you know what I'm saying."

"You and me, we were into each other right away. We fucked, and it was awesome, and we fucked some more, but even when we're not fucking, you make me laugh, and we can talk about boring stuff, but it's not boring. And when I kill somebody, you're okay with it."

"Not at first."

"But you are now, right?"

"Hey, I understand. We're Bonnie and Clyde on this thing."

"Dang, that's so old."

"But you know who I'm talking about. I should show you that movie, with Warren Beatty—"

Melissa pretended to fall asleep. Loud snore.

"Okay, okay, you win."

She laughed. "I've seen it. I saw it already. I'm not *that* young."

Then they were both quiet. The sun had sunk a little lower, and the orange was going red and purple. The lights were blinking on in the garage. They both knew there were around ten BGM soldiers hidden among the rows. More cars coming in than going out. It was dinner time for the retirees. The buffet awaited them. DeVaughn would've appreciated some himself right then. He would've admired Melissa as she ate. A real turn-on, watching a girl with a big ol' juicy ass enjoy a good meal. But not until this was over. And probably not even then.

He said, "I wished we had met some other time. I really do."

"Yeah, me too."

"You know what's going to happen next."

Getting too dark to read her face in the rearview. "You're going to kill Billy Lafitte."

"I wish it was that easy. He won't stand still while I do it."

"It's going to be loud, I bet."

"He can't get out of here this time. Lots of firepower. And when it's over, Motherfucker be dead."

"And so will those soldiers. And maybe me or you."

"Don't say it."

"But you know. You know how Bonnie and Clyde ended up, is what you're trying to say here, ain't you?"

DeVaughn felt chill bumps. Felt a lump in his throat. He couldn't picture Melissa dead. He remembered those car dealers dead on the floor. No, she couldn't end up like that.

He asked, "No chance of you getting the hell out of here, is there? Get far away from what's about to go down? I'll come find you. I promise."

"Thought you said Bonnie and Clyde?"

"Jesus, baby."

She squeezed tighter. "We kill him together. We get killed together. We escape together. I don't care. We stay us. We stay us, no matter what."

"I won't let you take the fall."

"Why not? You in jail, me in jail. I'm still your bitch in jail, you know. We'll get out one day. We don't have to be in the same room for it to be true love."

"Can't let you go."

She lifted herself from the seat, turned and kissed his cheek. "Then when the time comes, you'd better kill me, too. I'd rather today be my last day if you try to set me free while you go down."

"Baby—"

Another kiss, closer to his lips this time. Almost full dark outside except for the fluorescents. She kissed him. Wet, full, desperate. He gave it back to her twice as much. One more kiss before Billy Lafitte showed up to end this thing. DeVaughn would have to thank the piece of shit first. Without Lafitte, he'd have never met the love of his life.

And then he'd shoot Billy Lafitte in both his motherfucking eyes.

# CHAPTER TWENTY-THREE

Time made sense again once the docs began weaning Rome from the drugs. The pain was real but not overwhelming. He'd started to make words again. It was hard, but he sounded them out and forced his tongue and mouth to shape and push out syllables. He could ask for "water." He could ask for "TV news." He could ask for "Gillian," the cute nurse who reminded him of Desiree a little and who didn't look away when he struggled to speak and drooled all over himself to make himself understood.

Jesus! It was worse than living without Desiree, without his job, without having captured Lafitte. His leg, gone, yet still itched. His hands, fucked up, curling in on themselves. His nerves, alternating between "on fire" and "numb," made him feel as if this was an alien body. As if it had never been his to begin with, and he didn't understand the controls.

Day after day. Weeks. How long since Stoudemire had been here? He had no idea. Felt like ages, but was probably only yesterday. He couldn't keep the framework intact. He would hear the date on the news and then forget it. He would look out the window and realize it was still summer, at least.

Lost in time. Lost in space. Where had he heard the line before?

So he couldn't say exactly how long it was before

Stoudemire appeared at his bedside again, another pair of khakis and a golf shirt, another perfect head of spiky, bleached-tip hair. Legs crossed, an iPad resting on his thigh.

That fucking grin. "You're coming along, I hear? They say you can talk again?"

"Ffffff—"

"Don't strain yourself. We'll take it as it comes. But you've probably already guessed what you and Wyatt were doing was doomed from the start. Not to speak ill of the dead, but seriously, how was he going to help? This was Rock-and-Roll Fantasy Camp for you two idiots." He leaned forward, eyes darting around. He hoarsely whispered, "You want to know the rest, right? I think it might put your troubled mind at ease."

Was it really over? Had Stoudemire been able to pull it off? No fucking way. No *fucking* way. Rome had scoured the news, asked the nursettes to leave it on Fox News all day, knowing if Lafitte had really been taken down, it would show up there at some point, sensetionalists that they were on Fox. Of course Lafitte wasn't dead. He wasn't dead and he wasn't in jail. What was it Stoudemire was hiding?

Rome cleared his throat, said, "Tell. Me."

"Hey, not bad. You're going to be fine, you are. It's really a load off—"

"Tell. Me."

A nod.

Rome settled on his pillow, looked at the ceiling tiles and light fixtures. He cupped one hand over the other on his stomach, wishing he could interlace his fingers.

Something so simple, something he'd never had to think about before.

"I told you about Ginny Lafitte already, didn't I?"

Rome didn't move. Of course Stoudemire had already mentioned it. Shoved it in his face. He wanted Rome to feel guilty. It wouldn't work. Even without Rome interfering back then, Ginny Lafitte was already riding the suicide train. He had seen the ticket in her eyes, bought and paid for.

"We watched it all on security footage, everything except the final act, the murder itself. He parked a stolen motorcycle nearby, walked right into the facility, found a package to carry with him, fooled people into thinking he was a delivery guy, rode the elevator with several doctors and nurses, staring at their phones. He knew exactly which room Ginny was in, and he passed the package off to a nurse who, if she'd only been a little more curious, might have realized this 'delivery man' was all wrong, completely wrong." Stoudemire shook his head. "I mean, that's the rub of this job. We've seen it so many times, you can't help but get frustrated. It all adds up to trouble, but they can't see it. They only see pieces of it. Afterwards, we can't see the pieces without seeing the whole, where these idiots, they'll never see the whole. They'll never be curious enough. Knowing now what the nurse knows, even knowing that, she would still never see the whole picture."

It was hard to say, but Rome was determined: "Nah...*nah*...Oo. O. Nah-o. Lek-church. No lectures."

"I wasn't lecturing, buddy. Can't we discuss our operational philosophies? You know, the one I have actually works, based on years of experience, testing, and wisdom, and yours, which apparently relies on putting other people in danger to satisfy your own sick obsession?"

*Don't say her name.*

"Like Desiree?"

The lunge surprised Rome. It surprised Stoudemire, too. The look of pure fucking terror. Stoudemire shoved the chair back all the way to the wall in one slide. Rome was half-off the bed, twisted in wires, still reaching for Stoudemire, who was shouting for the nurses. It hurt like a motherfucker all over again, as if all his bones were snapping in twos, threes, and fours, but didn't Stoudemire look scared? Didn't it look as if he wanted his mama's tit to suck on again?

Good. Prick.

But that wasn't all. The nurses and nursettes wrestled Rome back into position and reattached the drip and the heart monitor and, fuck, so many wires. Stoudemire watched from behind them, arms folded, glaring. But once Rome was settled and the medical posse gone, Stoudemire picked up right where he'd left off.

About the mangled motorcycle they had found, the witness reports about the Cadillac, the man and woman shooting at the biker. The Caddy found abandoned behind a Wendy's, the car traced to DeVaughn Rose, the dead salesmen at the car lot next door, presumably killed by DeVaughn. The missing Tiburon. The fire at the home of Lafitte's step-parents. Lafitte's escape. DeVaughn's brazen car rental with his own credit card only hours after killing those car salesmen.

One thing Rome had noticed, though, was in Stoudemire's story, he still wasn't on the scene. It was all second-hand, or reconstructed via evidence. How late was he to this party?

Stoudemire took a breath, then said, "So, the shootout."

# CHAPTER TWENTY-FOUR

Blistered. Burning. Muscles cut ragged by a blade. Chest tight. Jaw tight. Left arm in his lap, throbbing. Goosebumps. Shaking.

Lafitte hit the ramp up the parking garage. Still in the Armada. So far, no cops. Might as well stick with it, because the fat kid, calling himself Lo-Wider, for fuck's sake, was a bitch to move, and he'd finally either calmed down or gone into shock. Quiet. Quiet was better. But before he had gone mute, he'd called DeVaughn and set up a meet. Didn't even matter if he had tipped off DeVaughn about having Lafitte with him. Must have been anticipating it anyway. Meeting in a parking garage. Of course.

Lafitte made the loops up to the third level, then slowed down. He saw BGM bangers sitting in their rides, slouched. Some more standing between cars, staring him down. Getting ready for the ambush. But that was not what DeVaughn wanted. He wanted this to be one-on-one. So they'd sit and watch, but ain't one of them would shoot first.

He turned to the passenger seat. He had the cop's gun. He had the little knife the little banger had stuck in him. He checked the glove compartment. Empty. So, yeah, one gun and a useless knife.

He lifted the gun, kept it low so the bangers outside couldn't see what he was doing. Goddamn, wrapping his taped-up hand around the grip was excruciating. He put all he had into curling his fingers, squeezed the trigger to the last possible millimeter before letting go. He dropped the magazine. Full. He sighed. This gun, fifteen rounds? Or fifteen plus one? He pulled back the slide—one in the chamber. Well...do the math.

"Hey, fat kid," he said.

Nothing but breathing from the backseat.

"Hey, I said." Lafitte reached back, slapped Lo-Wider's haunch. "You still with us?"

"*Leave me alone, you piece of shit!*"

"Good. So here's what's up. I'm going to kill your boss in a few minutes. I might get shot a lot while I do it. I think it's probably a good idea for you to stay down until it gets quiet. Then you can call for an ambulance."

"Fuck you."

"Or that. You can say and do what you want. I kind of don't care."

He eased the Armada around the corner and found DeVaughn's car, parked across three spots, him sitting there, window down and his gun arm out. Next to him, his girlfriend, grinning, practically witchlike. The more sinister she looked, the more attractive she was. Lafitte caught the shadows and corner-eye movements from more BGMs directly to his right, two of them in a Kia Soul. Was pretty sure he heard bass. Every ambush needed a soundtrack.

He stared at DeVaughn. DeVaughn stared back. The witch stared, too, and her grin turned into a smile, and then a laugh. She lifted her hands to show off her pistol, one much too large for her. But he wouldn't underestimate her. God no, he wouldn't underestimate anyone ever again. You never could tell.

So was this going to be a show? DeVaughn taking his time? Did he have a speech prepared? Maybe a photo of his brother to shove in Lafitte's face? Did he have a schedule for how this was going to work?

Fuck it.

Lafitte got out of the Armada, walked around the front of it toward the Kia Soul, lifted his gun and unloaded on both the bangers. The windshield exploded after the third or fourth shot and both those fuckers were dead and Lafitte dove inside through the hole he'd blasted right before the others started unloading on him.

He covered his head on the laps of the dead men while the bullets thumped into the engine block or tore through the backseat and back window. He scrabbled around feeling for the dead men's guns until he got hold of a Glock handle and tried to count back how many shots he'd blown through with his own. Seven. Yep, seven. He visualized it. Seven shots. Waited for a break in the fire, then hopped through to the backseat right before another wave started. He opened the back passenger door, kicked it until it wedged into the next car. He watched bullets take out the window and most of the plastic molding. He crept to the other side, slipped the door open more slowly, and snaked out onto the pavement and ran along the back of the row before they even figured out what had happened.

Stopped behind a convertible Chrysler, on his knees, warding off the pain and peeking beneath the car to see if they were heading his way.

Not yet. DeVaughn was out of the car now, shouting,

182

but the echo blurred whatever the fuck he was saying. Five more BGMs, out on the middle of the lot, holding guns the way they'd seen someone do in a *Fast and Furious*.

Lafitte had a gun in each hand. Probably twenty-three shots if he was lucky, if the banger had bothered to load his Glock to full-capacity. Another peek under the car. Two soldiers coming this way. Two headed behind the Soul. DeVaughn went back to his car, got in and closed the door. The witch started shouting at him. Goddamn.

Choices. There was a concrete column keeping the two farther down from seeing him. The other two, one doing the "duck under and look" thing now...maybe Lafitte could climb up on the bumper without—

"*Got him!*"

Then fuck it. Lafitte stood up and fired two-handed to make a lot of noise. Didn't hit either guy. He wanted them to scatter for cover. The Lincoln wasn't close. There was still fifteen, twenty feet of open pavement between him and it. Lafitte slid down by the car's front tire before the bangers rounded the column and the lead one squeezed off a few shots that blinged and flashed too close for comfort and scared Lafitte's heart into some deeper pain.

He shot back. One of the bangers said, "Got him trapped! Motherfucker trapped!"

Lafitte laid himself flat and scooted under the convertible. Then the next car. Then the next one, a truck, more headroom. He rolled. Gunshots and clinking and clanging and *GODDAMN* something bit into his leg. A concrete divot from a ricochet. He'd live. Crouching by the truck, he reached up, tried the door.

Open. It was big one, quad cab. It was a risk.

Lafitte popped up and laid down fire in both directions. The slide on the first gun clicked back. Empty. He opened the truck, crawled inside on the floorboard. It was a hotbox, Lafitte instantly soaking in sweat, stinging all those burns, as the bangers got a bead on him. More shots. Bullets popped through the windshield and side windows. Goddamn it, he was going to die in here.

So he screamed.

He screamed like he had nothing left. He screamed because his heart was in full attack-mode and he didn't know what else to do.

And then it got quiet.

His ears were ringing from all the gun shots. The bangers, they had to have felt the same thing. He opened and closed his jaw. He pinched his nose and blew. He *needed* to hear before they did. He *needed* to.

Finally got one ear to pop and heard, "Goddamn, son, you fucked him *up*!"

"How do you know he's dead?"

"Ask him."

"Fuck you mean, *ask him*?"

"I dunno, like, *ask him.*"

Goddamn. Lafitte was going to die in here.

"Hey!" One of the bangers, sounded close. "You alive?"

Lafitte rolled onto his stomach, on top of the guns. Why hadn't they shot him already? Why hadn't they finished him off?

Because DeVaughn, that was why. Same moment the thought bubbled up, he heard the bastard's voice telling his hired hard boys to "Back the fuck up!"

Lafitte stopped feeling so doomed. Seemed he had two choices.

One, he was going to die in here.

Two, he was not.


DeVaughn was just…just…just…*what the fuck*, man?

Wasn't supposed to be no James Bond bullshit. Was supposed to be *shoot him*. Was supposed to be get the motherfucker out the truck, then shoot him.

But what does Motherfucker do? He fucks it up. Because for all this talk about Lafitte, how he's some folk hero, some Superman, some kind of badass, it was a lot simpler. What it was was that Lafitte fucking cheated. He was a fucking cheater.

Wasn't no point in shooting all those BGMs. Motherfucker did it to make some noise, fuck up the plan. Couldn't talk to DeVaughn like a man. Had to find a way to make too much noise and now there was no time for anything. Gonna have cops and security all over the place, and, shit, now the motherfucker might already be dead.

Didn't Lafitte know better? Didn't he know how this shit was supposed to go down?

Melissa nudged him. "Go find out if they got him. At least do that."

"I bet they didn't."

"Well go find out before they fuck it up any more."

He sighed. He climbed out of the car. Watched the idiots trying to figure this shit out. Three of them, one at each end of the truck, and one heading for the blown-out driver's window, gun low.

DeVaughn's eyes went wide and he took a couple steps, but, shit, how stupid do you have to—

"Back the fuck up!"

The guy at the window jumped back quick. The other two laughed at him.

DeVaughn shook his head. "Are you all goddamned retarded?"

"But he ain't moving!"

"Because he's fucking waiting for you to get close so he can shoot you in the face."

The bangers looked at each other. Lost.

DeVaughn said, "Seriously, any of you ever been in a gunfight before?"

They looked around at each other again. Then the guy standing point in front said, "Have you?"

Fuck these motherfuckers. This was taking too long. "Just...stick your arm in and shoot him. Fucking shoot him."

The one nearest the door reached his arm in and before he fired, *something* grabbed his arm, pulled him in. Then his head exploded.

The other two jumped back, started firing low while backing up. Neither one had cover. DeVaughn watched the one behind the truck fall and scream. The other one hid two cars over, fired over the hood until he was out of bullets.

DeVaughn watched what happened next almost like it wasn't happening to him. Lafitte kicked out the busted up windshield and climbed out of the truck the same as he'd climbed into the Kia. He didn't worry about the bangers. Out of sight, out of mind. DeVaughn lifted his gun and fired and his hand jerked up and right and Lafitte kept coming. Picking up the pace.

"Shoot him!" Melissa shouting behind him. He couldn't help it. He looked over his shoulder and she was out of the car, getting ready to fire across the roof. DeVaughn blinked back to Lafitte and the fucker was almost on him, gun ready. DeVaughn fired from the hip and it was too late and Lafitte fired and got DeVaughn in the foot before slamming into him, going down hard to the pavement as Melissa got off her shot and missed. And three more in quick succession, *miss miss miss*. She screamed.

Lafitte slammed the gun barrel into DeVaughn's mouth and busted up his lips. DeVaughn scrambled and kicked and got his free hand around Lafitte's throat. Squeezed good and hard. Gonna rip the motherfucker's throat out. Dug in hard. Harder.

"You...goddamn...motherfucker!"

Lafitte pressed his chin down on DeVaughn's grip. He was starting to gag and growl. Lafitte swiped the gun at DeVaughn's face again, one, two, connected with the nose, with the jaw, three. DeVaughn felt his jaw explode again and thought for a sec Lafitte had shot it off, but it was the gun butt slamming into it. The banger who had run out of bullets had gotten his buddy's gun and was advancing, firing at them. Bullets ricocheted off the pavement and dug up rocks and then Lafitte jumped up, stomped dead center on DeVaughn's ribs, then his face, before swinging around, blasting—got the kid gangsta through the chest—and stumbling toward the Lincoln.

DeVaughn flipped onto his stomach in time to watch

Lafitte in the driver's seat, slam the door, and reach over to grab Melissa's leg. She kicked at him, but he got his arm wrapped around and pulled her down into the car. Motherfucker revved up and was gone. Tire squeal, all that noise, as the leftover bangers fired at the Lincoln as it sped down the ramp and DeVaughn shouted until his voice was raw, "No! No! No! Don't! You'll hit her!"

Then Melissa was gone. The Lincoln was gone. Lafitte was gone.

The ringing in his ears started to subside. Sirens.

The whole thing, all of it, took, what...four minutes? Four fucking minutes.

DeVaughn pushed up from the pavement, hurt like an assfuck all across his chest, and ran for the closest banger car, a pimped-out Toyota Camry, and climbed in back. "Go, let's go!" He fell back into the leather seat and closed his eyes, winced. Fucking Lafitte must've shot him in the heel or something. He lifted the shoe to his knee. Half the heel was gone, and there was blood, oh yes, there was blood. He clamped his teeth together and *Sssssssss.* Then his jaw lit up, too.

The car whirled three-sixty and shook him up, every jostle a jackhammer, and took off.

Fuck. Fuck. Fuck. Fuck. Fuck.

His phone rang. He pulled it out of his pocket. Melissa's name on the display. Jesus. Three missed calls in the last thirty seconds.

He answered, "Baby? Baby?"

Heard Lafitte's voice: "—up and sit still and it'll be okay."

DeVaughn: "You motherfucker! I swear, you touch her—"

"Gimme," Lafitte said. Then a struggle. Lafitte grunted, Melissa yelped, and Lafitte said, "Good. Now you won't shoot me."

The hell? "Hey, you'd better listen to me...Lafitte? You hear me?"

Then Melissa's voice, "I ain't got to shoot you. I'll let DeVaughn do that."

"He had a chance. A lot of chances."

"This next time, though, I swear. And then I'll cut your fucking balls off."

"Please. Shut up, please."

DeVaughn figured it out. Lafitte didn't know she had the phone. Didn't know DeVaughn was listening. Good girl.

"What's wrong with you?" She asked. "You going to pass out?"

Heaving breath. Lafitte caught it again, said, "I need...I need a doctor."

Well, goddamn. DeVaughn told the bangers up front to turn off the stereo and keep their mouths shut. He'd found a good one in Melissa. She could handle herself mighty fine. "Get out of here. I'll tell you where to drive in a few minutes."

*Give him somewhere to go, baby. Give him somewhere to go. I'll be right there waiting.*

# CHAPTER TWENTY-FIVE

By the time Stoudemire landed in Mobile to pick up the pieces after the attempt on Ginny, one of the local agents was there on the tarmac waiting, holding out a phone.

"Something happened in Mississippi."

Stoudemire took the phone from her and listened as another agent from the New Orleans office told him what had happened at the parking garage in Gulfport.

"A fucking war zone. But it was fast. By the time security got there, they saw two cars hightailing it. Three dead gang members, one wounded, and a shit ton of cars all shot up."

Stoudemire rubbed his mouth. He'd slept on the plane and was all dried out. He handed his water bottle to the agent and told her to open it for him. Then to the phone, "Where now? Last seen?"

"Best we got from the footage, it's a Lincoln Lafitte stole from another gangsta trying to kill him. The security chief at the casino says this guy is a regular, plays poker all the time, and does pretty good."

"No name yet?"

"I'm on the other line with him right now. I'll call you back."

The agent handed Stoudemire his water. He handed her the phone. "Thanks." Took down half the bottle in one swig. The heat down here. Good thing he'd dressed down. The agents in suits, fuck, no wonder they were always two steps behind whoever they were after.

"So," he asked the agent, who'd just told him her name. "Janice, you're driving?"

"Anywhere you need to go around town, they told me."

"Not anymore. We're going to Mississippi."

She rolled her eyes. "Fun."

"Don't worry." Stoudemire winked at her. "I hear they finally crawled out of the nineteenth century a few years ago."

"Stop," Rome said.

Stoudemire raised his eyebrows. "Something wrong?"

"Why...areyou...t-t-telling...methis?"

"What, about Janice? Janice is great. Here." He tapped his iPad then turned it for Rome to see. A blonde white woman, maybe in her forties, with brown eyes and a wide nose. That was all Rome could see of her because the bottom half of the photo was her mouth wrapped around, presumably, Stoudemire's cock. "Something to think about later tonight."

"Peessashit."

Stoudemire smiled. "In the bathroom of a New Orleans bar the next day. Nice."

Stoudemire filled in Janice on the drive to Gulfport, in-between phone calls to his wife, his personal assistant, and an agent he would need to cancel a boating trip with this weekend. He also laid the groundwork for fucking Janice—subtle questioning, the same way he could lead a husband suspected of murder to a confession was how he could lead any lady FBI agent to take her panties off.

Maybe it was the hair. Maybe it was because he first came across as gay. Couldn't help it. There was something about the "Southern effeminate" accent that drove women wild. He laid it on a little thick when the woman needed some persuasion, sure, but mostly it was a God-given bonus.

At the casino, Stoudemire skipped the parking garage, told Janice to give it the once over instead while he headed inside. He was tired of being hot as balls, and parking garages smelled like NASCAR pits. Instead, he was escorted to the security offices, given high quality coffee, a new ice-cold bottle of water, and was shown all four minutes and thirteen seconds of the shootout in dead silence. And then once again, stopping, rewinding, stopping. Then back to when DeVaughn Rose, professional poker player and ex-BGM gangsta, first pulled into the lot with two other cars and five bangers on foot only fifteen minutes before Lafitte had showed up.

"Got the plates?"

"Already out there."

Stoudemire nodded and turned back to the screen, watched one more time. He was impressed. He had forgotten how fucking *good* this Lafitte character could be. It was all improvised, firing at the Kia, jumping in, drawing fire, sneaking out. The truck, Jesus, Stoudemire was sure that was the end right there, but these BGM kids, Lafitte had picked up they didn't know exactly what they were doing. It was strategy versus testosterone. And down they went, one at a time. The fight with DeVaughn, fast and nasty. It was hard to watch, even harder than the prison riot tapes, Lafitte finishing off riot ringleader Ri'Chess by throwing him into the bonfire.

When it was over, Stoudemire sat, sipped his water, stared at the paused screen, Lafitte pulling the girl into the car.

"Have we figured out the girl yet?"

"A few possibilities," the police captain said. "We have a witness."

"A witness to what? The shootout?"

"He was in the SUV with Lafitte, in the backseat. Gunshot wounds, some burns. He says the girl's name is Melissa and DeVaughn only met her last night."

Stoudemire nodded. He stood, thanked the security people, and turned to the police captain. "Where is he?"

Lo-Wider was curtained off in the ER. He was crying light and low. The police captain and Stoudemire stepped past the guard, through the curtain, and found this kid handcuffed to the hospital bed. He was too wide for it, indeed. He was having a hard time balancing. He was all bandaged-up, especially the side of his head, a banger Van Gogh.

He looked at the cops and moaned a little louder. "I didn't mean anything. I was, I didn't, I mean, I didn't do anything."

Stoudemire smiled. "Sure you didn't, man. We're not up here for that."

Lo-Wider rattled the cuff. "Come on, man."

"For your own safety. Listen, you're the man right now. You're the guy. Tell us what you can about Billy Lafitte, about DeVaughn Rose, and this girl, what was her name?"

"Melissa," he said before Stoudemire was even finished. "Melissa. That's all I know. I think she worked at a truck stop. DeVaughn is crazy 'bout her. She's crazy, man, she's stone shit crazy."

"So why does DeVaughn—"

"Lafitte killed his brother, man! Shit, no wonder you can't catch Lafitte."

The police captain grabbed his phone, stepped out. Stoudemire heard him say, "See what you've got on DeVaughn Rose, or see if he has a brother, back in Katrina."

Stoudemire remembered this a little, something Rome had figured out about Lafitte and Asimov shotgunning a gangsta back in the day.

"What did Lafitte say?"

"He told me he was going to kill DeVaughn."

"Anything else? Serious, man, this could be your ticket to a free ride."

Lo-Wider started to shake his head, do the, "I done told y'all" shit, but then said, "He's hurt bad. His hair grease caught on fire. He's burned up, and, and, someone stabbed him, too, and, and, um, I think he's sick, too. He's acting sick."

"Sick how?"

"Sick, like, I don't know. Sick like my grampa gets sometimes. All hunched up."

Stoudemire gave Lo-Wider a pat on his foot, then stepped out to find the police captain still on the phone.

He said "Hold on," and pulled it from his ear. "Found him. Shabazz Rose. Unsolved. But, man, it was Katrina."

Stoudemire nodded, but was thinking about something else. Then he said, "I want to see his parents."

"DeVaughn's parents?"

"No, this fire. Lafitte's parents."

"Step-parents?"

"The fuck do I care? If they took him in, they might as well be his own blood. They should probably get tarred and feathered."

He called Janice, told her to pick him up out front. He waited for her inside the front doors, too hot to wait outside. Hard to believe he used to live down here, working the New Orleans branch. Never again. He was a D.C. lifer now, right up until it was time to retire to New Mexico.


Rome was exhausted after an hour of the story. Piecing it together on his own, a step or two ahead of where Stoudemire was going with it, took a lot of energy, especially when Stoudemire started on all the reasons he wanted to retire to New Mexico—"And the desert really isn't as hot as New Orleans, they tell me. Especially at night."

Rome waved off the rest, at least for the night. "Tired."

Stoudemire stopped talking and stared out the window. Rome wondered why he didn't get the hint. Time to go. The whole story, this giant tease, and he was at Stoudemire's mercy. The only way he was going to find out what happened next was to let the prick tell it his way.

Jesus, that blowjob pic. And for some reason, Rome had thought Stoudemire was a closeted gay. Rome wanted to laugh out loud. That would hurt. So he held it in. Still, Rome fell asleep thinking, once he got better, he would go find this Agent Janice and ask for the real story. Maybe he could even use it to get back on at the FBI. Maybe. *Maybe.* Maybes babies. Maybe rabies. Maybe someday...


Rome had to wait until nearly two p.m. the next day before Stoudemire showed up again, considerably less cheerful than before. It had been an excruciating morning—physical therapy, speech therapy, a bland lunch, an hour alone with the TV playing a rerun of a game show he was sure he'd already seen in 1987. Waiting was intolerable. It would have to be this way for a long time, wouldn't it?

Stoudemire didn't bother with taunting. He cleared his throat when he sat down and said, "The parents."

"St-t-tep-parents."

"Shut up, Frank."

"Sthere a...prow-blum?"

Another throat clearing. "Fine. It's fine."

*Liar. Terrible liar. Fucking liar.*

What did he have to lose? "Lie. Er."

Stoudemire looked away, out the window again. Rome tasted the apple juice from lunch coming up in his throat again. He burped. "Hear. Me? Lie. Er."

Stoudemire shook his head. "Why am I even bothering?"

Rome didn't say anything. Should he apologize? He needed to hear the rest of the story. He was *dying* to hear it. "Please?"

A firm nod from the prickly agent. Rome settled back on his pillow and closed his eyes.

He found Lafitte's step-parents at a neighbor's home, still exhausted after a visit to the ER for Jimena's burns, minor, and for possible smoke inhalation. Manuel had come home only a few minutes after Lafitte had head-butted the cop and taken off, two patrol cars in pursuit. The cops left at the scene were pissed off, so when Manuel came home and ran into the yard toward his wife, they tackled and tazed him.

"I expect an apology," Manuel said to Stoudemire. Even at the neighbor's house, there was a Biloxi cop standing at the archway between the kitchen and the dining room, where the couple sat alongside Stoudemire and Janice. The smell of aloe vera and coconut oil swirled around them. "This is ridiculous."

"Well, you do realize it was standard procedure. They had no idea—"

"Stupid," Jimena said. She seemed too cold, hugging herself, a man's flannel shirt draped over her shoulders. "You talk as if the cops are stupid. Or , ah, ah, robots. They knew. They were full of piss and vinegar. All because of Billy."

Manuel shushed her, laid his hand on her arm. Stoudemire watched him. A sad man, looking as if he had aged ten years in one hour. All the reports had shown a less-than-stellar relationship between Lafitte and his stepdad. Some might say Billy had learned a lot of his baddass bullshit from Manuel, made even worse by his hating Manuel.

But Jimena, she was the key. Stoudemire could tell. She had changed her husband's mind about life in general, about his stepson. About God and right and wrong.

"Billy's hurting," he said.

Manuel shushed again, barely a whisper this time. Jimena looked down at the table and nodded.

"He got burned, I know. And something else. I'm right, right? There's something else wrong with him."

Manuel said, "He'll be okay."

"You aided and abetted, you know. This is how you get your life back. You tell me what I need to know and we won't shove a hook through your lips and hang you out for bait."

Jimena barked a laugh. She unleashed a wave of Spanish. Stoudemire caught some of it—"Snakes, all of you, poisonous snakes," and "Fuck the police! Fuck them!" and "Santa Muerte will protect him."

Manuel sighed. In English, "She nearly killed him."

Jimena wagged her finger. "Not her fault! Not her fault! He's still alive, is not?"

Stoudemire sat back in his chair and waited it out. He turned to Janice. Another wink. This time she grinned. Going to be a good night, he could tell.

Manuel said, "They won't catch him."

Jimena seethed in Spanish under her breath. Stoudemire didn't catch any of it. She looked at the FBI agents and said, "What is it we have to tell you?"

"What's wrong with him? Who else could he go to for help? A way to get in touch—"

"No," Manuel said. "He's not stupid enough to keep a phone. We have no way to contact him. He won't come back."

"He was stupid enough to try killing his wife earlier today—"

"Ginny's alive?"

"Barely. Not exactly what you'd call 'and well', but breathing." Stoudemire's eyes lingered on Manuel an extra second. Why would that surprise him? Why didn't the 'attempted murder' part shock him? "He was stupid enough to come home at all. He's nothing but stupid, and he's going to die if we don't get to him first."

Jimena crossed herself. In Spanish, "God willing."

"Or he'll kill someone else, like this girl he took hostage. Or innocent people out on the road. He's done it before. He kills without thinking. You know I'm right."

Jimena shivered. Hugged herself again, rocked herself. Manuel stared at the table a long moment. Tapped his fingers on it. Tap tap tap. The air conditioner switched off. The sounds of the neighborhood seeped in. Kids playing on the street, only hours after the fire and the escape and all the cops, as if it had never happened. Manuel dug into the front pocket of his jeans and brought out a small bottle, set it on the table in front of Stoudemire.

"There's no one else to help him. He'll never get in touch again. That was the last time I would ever see my boy." Trying hard not to cry. Trying real hard. Brick of a face.

Stoudemire picked up the bottle. He knew what it was but wanted to be sure. Very small print on the bottle. He opened it, took a peek inside. Tiny white pills. Nitro.

Stoudemire said, "Thank you for your time." He meant it.

The plan was falling into place. But Stoudemire told Rome about it in a pissy voice with a pissy face.

Rome concentrated really hard and asked, "Why you mad?"

"Mad?"

"Pissy?"

Stoudemire glared at him, then looked at his watch. Seriously. Big hunk of a watch. When he looked up again, it was a pissy face showing off a pissy grin. "Maybe I'll tell you tomorrow.

He got up, walked toward the door, flipped off the light, and left.

Rome shook his head. "Prick."

# CHAPTER TWENTY-SIX

Lafitte had been preoccupied with the gun and with Melissa's flailing feet kicking him in the face. She'd lost a flip-flop at the garage. Kicking Lafitte's skull hurt her toes. He didn't notice she was dialing DeVaughn, praying he would answer. Several times. And finally, she saw he had picked up. She shoved the phone between her legs, up her dress, kept them loose so DeVaughn could hear everything.

Lafitte got the gun away. She told him how DeVaughn was going to kill his ass. Then he said, "I need a doctor."

Was he serious? Melissa said, "Sure, I'm a doctor. Here, give me the gun and I'll cure you."

Damned if Lafitte didn't grin in spite of himself. "Cute."

It was the first time she had gotten a look at him close-up. He was a mess. If there was anything appealing to him, it was hidden under burns, blisters, and scars. His hair was greasy, matted, and she could've sworn it was smoking. His hands and one arm were wrapped in duct tape. Loose skin on his face, neck and arms, angry and red underneath.

"What you need a doctor for?"

"I'm not feeling so good. If I promise not to hurt you, will you help me get one?"

"Fuck you. I hope you feel even shittier."

"How about this? I won't hurt DeVaughn either."

Whatever smartass remark she wanted to drop on him got frozen on its way out of her mouth. Not killing DeVaughn. Not that he *could* kill her man, just sayin'. Not that Lafitte had an ounce of DeVaughn's cold-bloodedness. But to not even try...

"Keep talking."

"You know why he wants me dead?"

"You killed his brother. You and some other cop."

Lafitte nodded. "Yeah, we did. He ripped us off on a drug deal. We were pissed off, and he was going to get the BGMs on our ass, so we found him, shot him, and dumped him into a ditch full of shit and mud and trash from Katrina."

She hoped DeVaughn had heard every word.

"Which one?"

"Hm?"

She said, "Which one of you shot him?"

"Paul had the shotgun. But fuck, I might as well have done it myself. The fucker tried to cheat us. I didn't flinch. Paul shot him in the chest, then walked up real close and shot his teeth out."

Melissa's mouth went dry. She couldn't swallow. She licked her lips, then said, "You'll leave him alone? You'll let me go and leave DeVaughn alone?"

He nodded, slowed down. He had gotten a lot of distance between them and the casino, heading north into the piney woods, looking to get lost down twisty two-lane roads. Melissa looked out her window. She could feel the vibrations of DeVaughn's voice against her thighs. She couldn't hear what he was saying, but knew it had to be, *Hold it together, baby. Lead me to you.*

*Keep him talking. I'm coming to save you.*

"Where are we going?"

"You tell me," Lafitte said. "Pull that phone out from your legs, hang up on DeVaughn and find me a doctor." He leaned over, spoke directly to her lap. "You hear me, DeVaughn? Loud and clear?"

When Melissa didn't reach for it, Lafitte did. Reached between her legs. She clamped her thighs together hard but he already had his hand around the phone and twisted his way out again. Shouted at it, "Your brother deserved it and I would do it again if I had to."

Ended the call. Handed the phone back to her. "You got three gee?"

She punched up a browser and said, "Like, a hospital?"

Lafitte shook his head. "A cardiologist."


When Lafitte hung up on him, DeVaughn let out a howl and then started slapping the driver's head.

"Stupid! Stupid! Stupid!"

The driver ducked and covered. "Hey, hey, hey!"

The whole time. He'd known the whole time. Probably didn't need no doctor either. Probably wasn't going to keep his promise to Melissa. DeVaughn was fucked. *Fuuuucked.*

He sunk back into the seat, phone loose in his hand, his fucking foot throbbing. Knew damn well his jaw was swelling up. Motherfucker. Lafitte killing his brother was one thing, but if the motherfucker dared even look at Melissa wrong...

His phone vibrated two short times. He took a look.

A text from Melissa: *Heart doctor.*

"Stop, stop driving! Pull over there." He pointed at the back of what used to be a Taco Bell, now painted white and blue and serving gyros. The driver hit the brakes too hard and skidded, got some horn attitude from behind, and pulled into the lot across two spots.

"Don't turn off the engine," DeVaughn said. "Leave the air on max. We've got time to kill."

He looked down at the phone and willed it to buzz again.

Melissa scrolled through names, said, "So, you need the address? Start at the top?"

Lafitte shook his head. He was driving one-handed, his left hand flat on his chest, all of him hunched close to the wheel. "Call them up, one by one. Ask if they're in today. First one who's not in, we look up his home address."

"Are you sure you don't want a hospital?"

"I don't want a hospital." He wouldn't look at her. She was glad of it, since his face straight-on was the stuff of nightmares right now. But she had to remember, he knew her every move. "Hospitals mean I'm outnumbered. Hospitals mean I get caught. The fuck do I want with a hospital?"

"They're also where you get fixed."

"What about the doctor's office? Why not there?"

"Same thing. Too many people. Too little control. I need a fucking doctor. You can be his nurse."

Melissa scrolled through. "You trust me? To just pick one?"

"No, girl, no. I don't trust you one bit. I trust the deal we made. I trust you believe me when I say if you fuck it up somehow, I'll kill DeVaughn. Might be a legion of cops descend on me at the hospital, but some way, somehow, DeVaughn would still die by my hand."

She did believe him. She sure as fuck did.

"Now, start calling doctors."


It was a long-ass time, sitting in that parking lot, smelling that sauce, tzatziki sauce, and the grilled meat smoke. DeVaughn's stomach growled. He should've eaten at Waffle House when he had the chance, but he was still getting over the dead bodies at the car lot. He wasn't mad at Melissa for it. The men had to be dealt with. But seeing them lying there, all dead and shit, it wasn't the same as he imagined standing over Lafitte's dead body would be. A jungle beast. A real prize. Something majestic. Not lumpy in a golf shirt and khakis.

The driver and friend tried to talk real low, like they didn't want to bother DeVaughn. One of them clicked the radio back on, picked up where it left off, a good beat. DeVaughn didn't know it. Sampled saxophone riff.

"Hey," he said to the driver. "Let me ask you. You know why I left, right? Why I left Mob?"

The driver shook his head. "Man, each his own. I do what I gotta do."

"But seriously." To the passenger. "You've got to know, right?"

The passenger was younger, maybe too young. Had a lot of spic in him. He had a goofy smile. "I never heard of you 'til this morning. You look like you get *paid*, bro-ham. Dollar bill, y'all."

The driver fought the giggle, then let it go. "Hold up, hold up, you ain't even shaving yet."

"Women like it smooth."

"You crazy, man." Then he turned to DeVaughn. "My brother knew your brother. Man, I'm sorry. I heard about it."

DeVaughn nodded. "Because, you know, there are times in a man's life...you can't carry that stuff around day after day. You want to compete at the level I compete at, you've got to let it go. You've got to, what, like, *meditate*. Clear your mind, try to read your opponent without him reading you."

The passenger shook his head. "I prefer dice."

"You have no idea what I'm talking about."

"I know. Don't listen to him." The driver looked in the rearview, caught DeVaughn's eyes. "We cool."

The phone buzzed. This time, a name and address.

"Alright, time to finish this."

Passenger: "You know it."

DeVaughn grinned but didn't let the kid see it. Eager beaver. Reminded him of...hey, where'd Lo-Wider get off to, anyway?


It took four tries. The first one, kids all over the yard. A couple of moms. Too much. The second, in a gated community, a rent-a-cop in the booth giving them a staredown as they drove past too slowly. The third, nobody home.

Melissa texted the first two names and addresses to

DeVaughn, but after those went bust, she wrote, *Wait. Working on it.*

They pulled up outside the house of the fourth, passed it, turned around, and parked on the opposite side of the street. It was an older neighborhood, not far from the beach, lined with ancient twisted oaks that had survived storm after storm, even Katrina. They looked painful, as if riddled with arthritis. They made the last of the daylight disappear, the darkness full-on now. Lights from the windows shone yellow, blurred. Lafitte blinked, rubbed his eyes. He was fading. It could be he was dying. Melissa had no idea. It didn't matter. DeVaughn would come and get her, and by then they would finish off Lafitte because her promise was shit. It was the only way she could live with herself, making sure DeVaughn got his revenge.

Lafitte took deep breaths, grunted, and finally got out of the car. He shoved both guns into the back of his jeans. Melissa walked around the front, following as Lafitte lumbered up the walkway. The house had a New Orleans vibe—stairs up to a wide front porch with columns. Everything white, only a little purple and gold in cushions for the outdoor furniture. The door was tall and looked heavy. Hanging plants with flowers over-flowing, same kind her grandma had. Purple petunias, pink geraniums, sweet and syrupy, like childhood.

Lafitte knocked on the door as if with a hammer, then leaned on it as if it had taken all his energy, let out a long breath. He waved her over with his chin. "Do the talking."

"What?"

"It's an emergency. Do the talking. Get us inside, at least."

Someone was coming to the door. They could see the shadow through the heavy glass, hear the footsteps on the wood floor inside. Melissa grabbed Lafitte's shoulders and pulled him upright as the man inside peered out the windows, unfocused and warbly.

He said, "Yes?"

Melissa shouted back, "I need help! My brother! He's having a heart attack! I need a doctor!"

Quiet. "How do you know I'm a doctor?"

"Across the street! Your neighbor said! She said you're a doctor! Are you? Can you help him? Can you? Please! It's been half-an-hour!"

The doctor opened the door while she was still talking, focused on Lafitte. "Can he walk?"

"Yeah, I'm good." Lafitte pressed his hand against the doc's chest and pushed him back inside the house. He pulled out one of the guns, and the doctor retreated, hands up. "Oh god, oh god. Wait, wait."

"You're Joshua Groff?"

He nodded. "Please."

"You're a cardiologist?"

Another nod. "Please."

Lafitte held the gun loosely in his right hand, the fingers of his left still spread across the doctor's chest. "Yeah, alright. You'll do."


By the time DeVaughn's crew rolled to a stop behind the Lincoln in front of Doctor Groff's house, the weak streetlights were glowing, and even more front porch lights. A quiet night in a rich, white neighborhood.

DeVaughn checked the text again to be sure. Melissa had added, *Think BL having heart attack.*

Seriously? What the fuck was a doctor going to do about it at his *home*? Did they all carry special "un-heart attack" shots for emergencies? DeVaughn remembered his dad had heart problems in his forties. Lafitte wasn't that old yet, was he? Then DeVaughn's dad died from a massive stroke at forty-nine. No one had ever explained what the deal was. His dad smoked all the time. Or maybe the stress at work did it. He had a hard job, Momma had said. Devaughn couldn't remember what it was, except Daddy wore overalls and smelled like Pine-Sol all the time.

Whatever. Blink the memory away and be patient. Think about the pain in your foot. The driver turned and asked what to do.

Hurt to talk. "Turn off the engine and sit tight for a while."

"Need back-up?"

DeVaughn shook his head. "Shit, I'm surprised you're both still here. Figured One O Four would want you to bring me in. I got a lot of BGM killed today."

"You kidding?" The passenger waved his phone. "He already texted. Said to do everything we can to help you get this son of a bitch. Got all sixty-three remaining BGMs ready at your command."

"Jesus."

"It ain't a DeVaughn Rose thing no more. It's family. BGM for life."

"Yeah." DeVaughn felt the weight of it. "BGM for life."

He held to the phone tight, waiting for Melissa's next buzz. Doctor Groff's front porch sure looked inviting. A man could really enjoy a warm evening and a cold drink on a front porch. Yes he could.

# CHAPTER TWENTY-SEVEN

When Stoudemire came back to Rome's hospital room the next morning, he was all business again. Suited up instead of casual. His silk tie must've cost him a cool hundred bucks. He smelled like expensive cologne, which didn't smell any better than cheap cologne. He took his seat beside Rome's bed and sighed.

"I've got to finish quickly. I have to fly back to Washington."

"Why?"

An ever-so-slight sneer. Stoudemire sucked on his teeth. Awful sound. "I know you'll find out anyway. Janice must have told someone about us, a friend, maybe. The friend, I don't know, some uggo who got jealous, or some guy who hadn't gotten as far as I had with her, went and told her SAC. I'm getting called back to Washington for a meeting. A fucking meeting. Waste of time."

"But..Lafitte?" Hard to put more than two words together, still. He'd have to push harder during therapy. "Lafitte?"

"Yeah, Lafitte...I've got forty-five minutes. Here it is."

First, the hospitals. No luck.
Then, the free clinics. Still no luck.

211

Doctors' offices? Nope.

Veterinarians? Negative.

When the FBI wanted to, it could move at lightning speed. And goddamn it, did it ever want to. Lafitte, back home on the Coast, hobbled, with blood on his hands, literally. He would get the death penalty this time, if he made it that far. More likely, death by cop, right here, right now.

Stoudemire, Janice Moore, and Captain Delaney were each on their own phones, talking to three different sources, all at once. It was cacophony in the car. They were driving aimlessly. No one had a lead. No one had the Lincoln yet. No one had an idea.

After another wasted call, another report of nothing-fuck-all-nothing, Stoudemire hung up and rubbed his temple. He really wished Delaney wasn't here. A blowjob from Janice would have been great right then. It would've helped him think. He thought he had her on the hook. His suggestion for dinner had gotten a "We'll see" and a smile. Still, if only the cop wasn't in the backseat...

How did Lafitte think? As much as Stoudemire hated Franklin Rome, he was the one guy who knew how Lafitte thought. After their first tangle, Rome had been smart to finagle a transfer to New Orleans. Almost had the bastard, too. Knew which bait to use. But then it went to shit. Everything involving Lafitte eventually did. It was inevitable. It had been fourth and inches in Sioux Falls, cornering Lafitte and Steel God in a hotel, one second left on the clock. And then Lafitte had killed Rome's wife. It didn't matter that they'd caught him and thrown him in jail. It didn't matter that Rome had gotten a lot of the credit, since further investigation showed he had gone rogue in a bad way. All of it was moot once Rome had sent that bitch Colleen Hartle into the prison for revenge and instead had stirred themselves a prison riot, a dead boy, and Lafitte on the run again.

But goddamn if he couldn't get inside Lafitte's white trash mind. Kind of amazing, actually. Still, he threw Hartle under the bus, and got himself a terribly nice severance package because, well, he knew too much. He'd played a smart game. He'd lost badly, but goddamn, he was the best sore loser Stoudemire had ever seen.

One phone call to Rome. Just one. Might save him hours. Might save lives. But all that invalid could do was drool at him.

*Fuck Franklin Rome. I got this.*

"He's not going to the hospital." Mumbled it. Janice heard, stopped talking. Stoudemire looked over at her. "Well, he's not, right?"

"I'll call you back." She ended her call, as did Captain Delaney in the back. He pulled himself closer, chin on top of the passenger seat.

Stoudemire said, "He won't go to a clinic. Won't go to the ER. So, where?"

"Drugstore?"

Stoudemire shook his head. "The employees would trip the alarms instantly. And there are cameras."

Delaney said, "There are cameras everywhere."

"Maybe. Maybe not."

"What's that supposed to mean."

It was so clear. This was kind of easy. Fuck Rome again. "He won't go where the doctors work, but how about where they live?"

Janice said, "Why would he do that?"

"He's not looking for surgery. He's looking for a diagnosis. Instructions. Someone to tell him what to do next."

Delaney went *hmph*, then, "Then how do we find out…"

Stoudemire looked at Delaney in the rearview. "Yep. All of them."

Rome tried to laugh. Sounded bad.

Stoudemire cleared his throat. Then, "He hadn't shown up at any hospitals, ERs, or clinics, but we knew he wouldn't. We had to cross them off the list. We called as many heart doctors as we could, and ended up with four who didn't answer the phone, and three more who sounded suspicious."

Rome shook his head. "No. Wouldn't answer."

"You're right. I thought the suspicious ones were worth checking out first. I wasted a lot of time and manpower."

Rome wanted to tell him it was okay. Making mistakes was how you learned. But telling him would take too much effort in his current state, and the last thing he wanted to do was be *sympathetic* to this piece of shit. It was also the first time since the crash Rome realized that not only would he survive this whole ordeal, but he'd thrive. Goddamn, he might even have a chance to get back into the action, especially if Stoudemire was the best they could throw at Lafitte these days.

"We cleared all three," Stoudemire said. "Two were

having affairs at the time. The third...he'd scored some meth a couple of hours before."

Rome could've told him. Don't pick up rocks if you don't want to see the bugs underneath. Except that's what they were paid to do, pick up rocks all day long. Just so happened Rome was better at picking up the right rocks.

"Joshua Groff." Janice read the name of the last doctor who hadn't answered their call. The other three had been accounted for. So here it was. "What now?"

Stoudemire knew the right answer. This was textbook. Now was the time to call in a full-on SWAT team to descend on the neighborhood and secure it. Somehow find out who was in the house and where inside it. Get in contact with Lafitte if he was in there, make sure he understood his situation. Play it patiently. Cover every angle.

But goddamn, if he turned out to be wrong...

"Let's mosey on over. A drive-by."

Janice turned to him, squinting. "Sir? Really?"

He wagged his finger-gun at the windshield. "Make it so."

Rome started laughing for real. It had been a while. Tears. Stoudemire's cheeks glowed. Looked like he was sucking a lemon. The man had just explained he would prefer to take a chance and be proven right in front of the agent he wanted to fuck and the local police cop rather than go for the safest and best. All because he didn't want to be wrong again. It was really funny. Fucking hilarious.

Stoudemire stood, buttoned his suitcoat. "I've got to take a piss. You'd better get it out of your system by the time I get back."

He walked over to the bathroom, Rome still laughing, even pointing at him to really twist the knife. But once he closed the door, Rome took some deep breaths and wiped his chin on his shoulder. Stoudemire could've shut the whole thing down right then. Why hadn't he? Why take all the abuse if he didn't have to?

It could only mean one thing: they *needed* Rome.

They sure did.

Crawling back, begging for his expertise.

And he loved it. He would tell them no, of course, because then they would either leave him alone, or they would offer him something he couldn't refuse.

Either way, he would be celebrating later with a juicebox.

# CHAPTER TWENTY-EIGHT

It was a first for both of them. Lafitte had never explained his symptoms to a doctor while pointing a gun at him. The doctor had never listened to a patient explain his symptoms while having a gun pointed at him. Once he was done, Lafitte couldn't help but mumble, "Sorry."

Doctor Groff had already told them he was alone in the house. He and his wife were separated, trying to work through things, and both of his kids were in college at LSU. One a freshman, one a senior. It was him all alone in the big old house right now. If he was telling the truth.

Each step Lafitte took further away from shore, the stronger the riptide. He had fucked himself in too deep. Could he trust Melissa to check the rest of the house for him? Could he trust the doctor to get him some nitro? Could he trust both of them together if he sent Melissa to watch Doctor Groff while he got the nitro?

Aw, fuck it. Lafitte sat on the stairway, leaned against the bannister. "Help me, please."

It was Melissa who acted. She took the gun from Lafitte and trained it on the Doctor. "Let's get him something. We don't want to hurt you. But I swear to fucking Jesus himself, if you don't help—"

"I'll get some nitro. Follow me. But please stop with the gun. I'm a doctor. Do no harm? Remember?"

"Good for you. I've already killed people today. I do plenty of harm. Don't piss me off."

They left the room and Lafitte smiled, shook his head. Might as well tie on his own toe-tag, letting them go off together.


Melissa followed Doctor Groff, giving him space so he couldn't turn and surprise her, disarm her. He whispered at her the whole time over his shoulder.

"He's not your brother is he? We can help him and still help ourselves, you know. If you put the gun away."

"He's not my brother. But I have to do this."

"Seriously, he's in no shape. We can call for help, real help."

They stepped into his home office, lined with half-full bookcases, plaques, framed photos of a normal doctor with pretty wife and well-tended children when they were younger. Nothing recent. The only books she recognized were a line of John Grisham hardcovers next to a line of Michael Crichton hardcovers.

He started to walk behind his desk when Melissa blinked and lifted the gun straight and said, "Wait, get back, get back."

He stayed put. Hands kind of up, kind of not. "I have nitro and aspirin in my desk."

"I'll get it."

"But they're right—"

"Shithead, I said…" Then she made some exasperated noise and pushed him aside, checked the drawer herself. Yep, there was a gun. A fucking .45. She looked up at him.

He stared away at the floor.

"Where is the fucking medicine?"

"You know," Wouldn't meet her eyes. "If you and I both had a gun...I swear I can help you both."

She thought for a second. DeVaughn should be waiting outside by now. Anything that didn't end with him killing Lafitte was bad for them both. For a moment, she thought about killing the doctor. He was right. There was nothing he could do except hand over a few pills and tell Lafitte he really needed to go to the hospital.

She really thought about it. One shot. But she felt sad inside. She missed DeVaughn already. The plans were all bullshit now because Lafitte had to go and fuck it up. So why not kill the doctor and tell DeVaughn to join the party.

Instead she said, "Get the fucking medicine and don't play me again."

The whole thing was a bad board game, the kind she'd always got stuck playing with her family on Thanksgiving. It sucked, but they'd come this far. Might as well roll 'til the end.


Lafitte couldn't believe it. They came back. Letting them go had been a gamble, but he had this idea Melissa was saving him for DeVaughn. It wasn't long, only a couple of minutes, the doctor carrying a tiny vial with a screwtop cap, which he had opened and had shook a pill into. He handed the cap to Lafitte. Itty bitty pill.

"Drop it under your tongue and let it sit there. Don't pick it up. Drop it in."

Lafitte did. "Then what?"

"Don't, no, don't talk. Let it dissolve. Sit still. Relax. Take deep breaths. If this is really angina, you should feel better soon. If it's a full-blown heart attack, we really need to get you to a hospital."

Lafitte squeezed his eyes tight and waved his hand randomly. "No hospital. No. No. Something else. No hospital."

"Breathe through your nose. Easy, deep."

While he did his best, Melissa asked the doctor, "If he won't go to the hospital, is there anything else you can do?"

A long, soft sigh. The doctor's voice was trembling. His throat was dry, every word like sand. "Listen, are you listening? Please. I can't tell you anything until I do an angiogram. We need to look at the arteries, find out which ones are the problem. And from the look of you, I don't think we have long. Is there a history of heart disease in your family?"

"Look, she's not my sister." Lafitte said. "I'm Billy Lafitte. I'm sort of famous. And, honestly, yeah, maybe there's been heart trouble in my family. I haven't kept up with them, though. Been years and years. And I'm pretty sure mine's due to steroids."

The doctor took a step back. "Jesus."

"What?"

"You need an EKG."

"No, what I *need* is a diagnosis without going to a fucking hospital. Weren't you *listening*? Fuck's sake, I'm a wanted man."

The doctor shook his head. Sweating bad. "I'm sorry, I'm sorry, but, there's nothing I can do here. I need, I need, I need, um, machines, computers, equipment. A catheter. I need the dye so we can see. You might need, uh, maybe a stent. It's complicated."

"What's wrong with me? Start there. What is it? Give it a name."

"Steroid users, weightlifters, serious athletes, they get what's called Left Ventricle Hypertrophy. You've got crazy high blood-pressure, I bet. It means the walls of your ventricle are thicker and not pumping well. Usually we can fix it with meds, and you'd have to stop steroids completely, obviously. If you've been on the juice for a long time, maybe the damage has spread."

"What meds? Do you have them? Can we get them?"

"Jesus, it's *not that easy!*" The doc's voice jumped in volume, pitch. Goddamn fidgety hands. "I can't tell you anything without an EKG. I need to do this properly."

"Melissa, shoot him, okay?"

She looked shocked at first, but then two-fisted the gun and lifted it and—

"Hey!" Lafitte shouted, held up his hand. "Whoa. I want to scare him."

"But you said—"

"I said shit! You're not paying attention. I didn't say kill him, I said shoot him, but I didn't even mean it. Fear motivates people. Death just kills them. Shit, girl."

She lowered the gun, one handed. Put her free hand on her hip and cocked it out. "So now he knows you don't want to kill him. Great."

"He knows *you* will, though."

The doctor backed into the wall hard enough to shake the antique crap on the table next to him. He slid down. "Stop it! Please stop it! What do you want me to do?"

Lafitte stood, couple of steps, leaned over him. "I

want you to *fix me*. I want you to fix me and let me slip the fuck away so I can keep out of fucking jail, alright?"

The doctor held his arms over his head, openly panting now. He asked, "Are you feeling better? Now? Are you?"

"The fuck you talking—"

"The nitro! Did it work? How do you feel now?"

"Well, shit." Lafitte rose to full height, what little there was of it, and placed his palm on his chest, rubbed circles. "A little better. It's not so much...pressure."

He stepped back, turned to Melissa and reached down for the gun. She tried to hold on, a little pout on her face, but he wrenched it free. Melissa crossed her arms and stalked away, kept her back to him.

Lafitte stood still, head low, hand still on his chest. He thought calm thoughts—snow, sunset over the Gulf, more snow, a lazy day on a pier, fishing for flounder, more and more snow. He hadn't realized how much he missed snow, especially after it nearly killed him. There was still pain, and now he had a headache all the sudden, but it wasn't so *right there*. It wasn't so *shit fuck goddamn*. It was *take five*.

He lifted his chin. The doctor was still on the floor, knees up, arms wrapped around them. Lafitte said, "Please. Tell me what I need. You don't have to get it for me. Just tell me."

Doctor Groff couldn't look him in the eye. He was shivering too much. "Blood pressure drugs. And and and a, um, B-beta blocker. And *aspirin*, yeah, baby aspirin. only one per day. And and and nitro, yes, nitro, only if the pain is bad. Only when it's bad. Unbearable."

Lafitte nodded. "What else?"

The doctor cleared his throat, got his nerve back. "Worst case scenario? You need a bypass. Or a stent. Bypass is better. You need to rest. You need to turn yourself in and get some help."

"Yeah, probably." He grinned. "Good advice."

"Please, please, I won't tell anyone. I promise, if you'll both leave, I won't say a word."

"Why not? It's a damned good story, ain't it?" He turned to Melissa. "So where is DeVaughn now?"

Melissa shrugged. "How should I know?"

"Because you've been texting him. I've been letting you. So where is he?"

She looked over her shoulder. "You promised."

"I did."

"Okay. Okay. I think, I mean, I guess..." A glance toward the front door. "He says he's right outside."

"Okay. You tell him what I promised. You tell him I'm bringing you out. You tell him I'm going to let you go as soon as I know I'm free and clear. Got it?"

Another pout, this one harder. The rocks on this chick, right? She said, "He would've won, you know. He would've. You cheated. The only reason you're walking out alive is because you're a cheater."

He waggled the gun, not really at her, but still. "Just, just, text the motherfucker already, will you?"

# CHAPTER TWENTY-NINE

Other BGM cars were moving into place, up and down the street, parking on curbs. They couldn't stay there for too long without scrutiny—black men parking in front of *my* house? Got to be up to no good, you hear me? *No. Good.* But for the moment, they were taking up every available bit of concrete the street provided.

Shit, the little man didn't short DeVaughn. This might be the whole goddamn BGM army dripping in one pimped ride at a time.

Then the text. The heartbreaker. *Lafitte say He wont kill U. He'll let me Go and wont kill U if U dont kill him.*

That fucking white boy. Smart fucking white boy. DeVaughn rubbed his neck, bruised from Lafitte's grip. One of them "do or die" type situations. One of them "damned if you do" type lessons. He slumped into the seat, barely at eye level with the window. He wasn't up for another chase. This was the moment. This was the last chance to catch this nigga-killing pig by the toe. Thumb and forefinger still at his throat, rubbing, rubbing.

Sure, tell Lafitte it sounded fine. Tell him he wasn't going to kill him. As soon as Melissa was in the clear, unleash those BGM bangers to finish him off. Not as satisfying as doing it himself, but at least he had a front-row seat to the show. In fact, there was no question. *No* question. He couldn't let any harm come to Melissa.

He'd slap fallen in love with the bitch, and now there wasn't nothing he could do about it. The heart wanted what the heart wanted. Okay, maybe the heart had a little help from the cock, but love was love.

He texted back, *Yea. Come on out, Baby.*

Another car passed by, caused DeVaughn to look up. This one wasn't BGM. This one was white people. Three of them, looking over at the doctor's house. Slowing down. What, were they dinner guests? But they didn't stop. They drove on. Just spying on the neighborhood. Envying what their neighbors had, most likely. Such a lush lawn. Such a nice boat. Such a nice antique door. Fuck's sake. Make this kind of money, get yourself a *new* door, man. Don't take no sloppy seconds.

The car drove on, riding its brakes until it turned into a driveway farther along. DeVaughn shook his head and texted Melissa again. *Come to Daddy, Baby. We've got living to do.*


Janice passed the empty Lincoln and said, "That's the one we want. Plate matches."

She slowed down in front of Doctor Joshua Groff's home, all bricks and pillars, stepped right off the screen of *Midnight in the Garden of Good and Evil* with Kevin Spacey. Stoudemire expected most of the Southerners he met to act like Spacey's caricature. The problem with Washington, D.C., was that even though people *say* it's a Southern city, everyone in it is from somewhere else.

"Nice place."

"Mm hm," Janice said.

She slowed, then kept on easing down the road.

"Quiet."

The Captain poked his face between the seats again and said, "Either one of you notice the shit ton of gangbangers lining this whole street?"

Stoudemire turned his head a fraction. He didn't want to make it obvious he'd missed all the other cars. A lot of them, actually. More than expected. And yeah, some dark figures silhouetted in each. "Don't let on that we see them. We're out of our element here."

Delaney said, "Jesus. This is going to be a massacre."

Fuck! If he had just ordered the SWAT team. How many more mistakes would he make tonight? Fu-uh-uh-uck. "Look, it's…we can…Janice, turn around up here. We'll make another pass. I'll get some back-up."

He started on his phone while Janice pulled into someone's driveway next to a covered boat and a Lexus SUV. She parked, backed up, turned left for another pass, then hit the brakes hard. "Holy shit!"

Stoudemire looked up. Whoever he had dialed was saying, *Hello? Hello, anyone there?* His eyes went wide. "Un-fucking-god-damn-believable."


DeVaughn got out when he saw Lafitte walk through the front door, at first seeming to drag Melissa out of the house, but then realized it was both of them dragging the doctor out with them. After shoving him down the steps into the yard, Lafitte pointed, said, "Stay" to the doc as if he was a dog, and then gently pulled Melissa in front of him, a human shield, and eased toward the road. He held a gun against the small of her back. DeVaughn held his hands low and out, like a Western gunfighter. He thought better of it. Crossed his arms instead.

"Jesus, Billy. Look at you."

"Quite a sight?"

"Son, that's going to leave scars."

There was a hint of a grin. "They'll cover up the old ones."

DeVaughn felt his gut tighten. He thought back to the truck stop, seeing the man for the first time in years. Battered, sure, but still a solid man. His shorts and workshirt combo had strained at the seams a little, and his hair, a fucking mullet, the man trying to hold on to his glory days when he had roamed the streets with *Girls, Girls, Girls* in the tape deck. Seeing him now, not even forty-eight hours later, how was the man still standing? Duct-taped together, his hair burned away in patches, what was left all melted-looking. DeVaughn was surprised to not see Terminator-metal under torn skin. How did this motherfucker do it?

"So what's this I hear about your heart? Is it broke?"

"It'll kill me before you will, that's for damn sure."

They both laughed.

Lafitte asked, "Your girl told you what's up?"

DeVaughn nodded. "Swinging your big dick, telling her you won't kill me. Bitch, I'm not the one needing protection."

"We all know your dick is bigger than mine, DeVaughn."

"Damn straight."

DeVaughn looked at Melissa, who was all pissed. He wanted to tell her it was all okay, and that Lafitte wasn't going to leave this town alive. He'd told the driver to get these BGMs on the phone, tell them as soon as Melissa was free, *somebody* better make Lafitte dead right quick. "Here's what I want," Lafitte said. "I'm taking her over to the Lincoln. She's going to shield me while I get in. Then I'm going to slowly back the fuck off this street. Then we are never going to see each other again."

DeVaughn had to smile. Had to shake his head. "Shit, man. Whatever you say. You won. You sure did."

"Let's call it a draw."

"You've still got one point in your favor."

Lafitte sidestepped toward the Lincoln. Very slow, very deliberate. Melissa had her head back, taking baby steps, tripping up Lafitte. She said a little loud, "Baby, you really going to let him get away?"

"Hush, now, we'll talk about it later."

"I mean, he's *right here.* I can duck."

Lafitte eased his arm over her shoulder, across her chest, hand hovering above her breast. "Easy now. Almost over."

DeVaughn said, "I'm sorry, baby. This is one of those things a man's got to do for love. What was that song? I'll do anything for love, but I won't do that?"

"Meat Loaf?"

"Something like him, yeah. Well, baby, I *will* do that. I swear to you."

Not far from the car now. Maybe six, seven more steps. Soon as she was free, the boys would unleash on Motherfucker. Lafitte said, "This is all real sweet."

Did he really not see he was surrounded?

Another minute, this would be over.

But then the car with those white people turned around in a driveway and started back. Rolled about ten feet and then slammed on its brakes. Headlights blinding them and shit. DeVaughn lifted his hand and squinted and those white people got out of the car, all of them pointing guns this way over the tops of the car doors.

The one on the passenger side shouted, "Don't move! Any of you! Don't! Fucking! Move!"

And DeVaughn right in the middle. He held his hands up, one in each direction. "Now, wait a minute. You *know* I didn't have nothing to do with this one, Billy. You let go of Melissa like you promised and get yourself out of here."

"It's FBI," Billy said. "I think that guy's FBI."

The FBI guy shouted, "I will cut you the fuck down! We've got the neighborhood blocked off! There is no way out, Lafitte. This is it!"

DeVaughn didn't know if he should hit the ground or make a deal with Lafitte or what. He let the fear ride him for another moment. If there was an FBI man pointing a gun at them, it meant there was all sorts of hell on the way.

"Lafitte," he said. "I run interference, you take Melissa and get on out of here. Deal?"

Lafitte was frozen. His grip around Melissa's neck was tighter and she was trying to pull his arm away. She was bending backwards as he dragged her along.

"Jesus, Billy! Are you listening?"

The FBI man shouted, "She's not dead, Billy! Ginny is not dead! Do you hear me?"

Jesus. Even DeVaughn wasn't ready for that.

He took a step closer to Lafitte and Melissa. "I thought you...I thought...She was the only reason..."

Lafitte's grip on Melissa loosened. But he still had his gun in her back. His arm over her shoulder, more like she was helping to hold him up. "Man, I don't know. I couldn't do it. Thought she was going to do it herself. I'm too tired."

"Give up now!" FBI again. "Give up now and you can see her. She's not dead, Lafitte!"

Car doors opening. DeVaughn looked around as the BGM bangers all climbed out of their cars, all strapped and showing, ready for war. Jesus. *Screaming* for a white boy to shoot one of them. He ducked his head and held his hands higher. "Hold up! Hold your fire! Now, now, let's talk about this."

"Ain't no talk to talk," said one of the BGM soldiers, tall with crazy long arms draped over the top of his car door. "One O Four said we're here to kill Billy Lafitte, and nothing you say is going to change that. If we got to kill cops to do it, so be it."

"Jesus, no, listen, this is *my* hit. My call! I'm the one who told One O Four to send y'all!"

Shook his head. "Yeah, he said you might get cold feet. Said if that happened, kill the motherfucker anyway."

DeVaughn looked back at Billy. "Now, listen."

Lafitte ground the barrel of the pistol harder into Melissa's back. "Thought we had a deal."

"You're a smart white boy. You know the rules. Chess, man. Chess. Got to think ahead."

"Oh, I did."

"Did you, now?"

"Got you in check."

"Shit, boy, that mouth of yours."

More shouting from the FBI guy, but it got lost in the wind and the echoes of sirens still too far away.

* * *

As soon as Stoudemire saw who it was standing in the street, he dropped the phone mid-dial and grabbed for the door handle. Janice and the Captain followed suit, but shit, both of them made protests and "Are they coming?" and "This is a bad idea" and shit, but fuck them. This was *the moment.* All of Stoudemire's Chuck Norris dreams were coming true.

Out of the car. Shouting. He couldn't hear himself, but hoped it sounded fucking badass. It was only then he realized there was no back-up yet. What was he supposed to do, call time-out and get his phone?

"Janice," he seethed through his teeth. "Call for backup."

"What? I thought—"

"You've got Bluetooth. Goddamn it, mine didn't go through."

"Right now? Right fucking now?"

"Jesus." They should've driven a little closer. Too far out right now. Lafitte could run for it. And DeVaughn, standing between them because Lafitte had his girl, this was so fucked up. But *the big three* standing right there! This never happened. Never.

"Do it, Janice. Make the call and I'm telling you, you're D.C.-bound. Consider this your interview for a big promotion."

She stared at him, wide-eyed, but then crouched and made the call.

The Captain said, "I don't know if this is a good—"

"Hold steady. We've got this."

More shouting at Lafitte and DeVaughn. Then he

blurted it out, about Ginny still being alive. Not very alive, but alive anyway. If Lafitte knew, maybe it would change the outcome. Delaney and Janice both stared at him. *Are you nuts?* But Stoudemire knew, time and time again, Lafitte's whole psyche revolved around that woman.

"She's still alive, Lafitte!"

Then sixteen car doors opened and sixteen BGM bangers got out, some standing, waiting, some aiming guns at Lafitte, and some more aiming guns at Stoudemire's car.

What would Chuck Norris do? What would *Walker, Texas Ranger* do?

Stoudemire was a smart man. He knew the answer.

Chuck would yell, "Cut" and head to his trailer.

Goddamn it.

# CHAPTER THIRTY

The nitro was wearing off. Lafitte was paining bad. Real bad. So the doctor might have been right. His heart was fucked. Only chance to save it was hit the hospital. He was pretty sure the FBI guy could get an ambulance for him. Lafitte alive was a much bigger fish than Lafitte dead.

And then the FBI guy said *Ginny was alive?* The fuck?

She hadn't gone through with it? They'd stopped her before she finished? Had she rolled over on him, given him up this time? Jesus.

He glanced back at the doctor on the grass, on his phone now. Shit. Would he still help keep Lafitte alive until the EMTs showed up? Wasn't that his oath? Lafitte was getting angry thinking about what would happen next. Fuck. He hated this, *hated* it, feeling helpless. Hurting so bad he would gladly hand over control to the doctors and the police. The last time he'd felt this helpless was when his son died, right in front of him, and there was no one to help then. No cops, no doctors, no god, no one.

But now, Ginny still alive, if he turned himself in, it would be a fucking circus. Would she testify against him? They'd force her to. They had leverage. They'd make damned well sure she remembered her kids. They'd make sure she knew Ham was dead and it was all Billy's fault. Goddamn. He couldn't turn himself in now. So

233

close to some relief, and this asshole had to tell him Ginny wasn't dead.

Another bolt of pain, an electric eel in his arm. He tightened up on Melissa and she gagged. She said, "Please." He let up a little. Cold sweat on his back while Melissa's warm body smothered his front. Having a hard time keeping hold around her neck, her literally bending backwards. She could take him in his current state, so he needed to keep the pressure up, make her believe she couldn't. The gun in her back helped. This girl, man, if she thought she had an opening, she'd go for it. Not sure what DeVaughn saw in her, what she saw in him, but shit, Lafitte could *feel* the vibes there. DeVaughn would die for her, and she would kill for him. True motherfucking love.

Then the BGM boys climbed out of their cars. And those motherfuckers were not going to let him get away this time.

Plan B.

There was no Plan B.

He needed to improvise. It sucked, too. Good chance it wouldn't fucking work. Good chance it would give him nightmares. He was long past remorse for killing. This game, everyone who played knew the rules, right? But that didn't mean there weren't nightmares. Got to deal with them was all. Got to deal.

He thought about the Santa Muerte candle. He thought about it igniting his hair. He thought about how sometimes Death giveth, and sometimes it taketh away.

"DeVaughn," Lafitte said. "I've got one more thing to say to you."

"Please, man, please."

"Your brother, us killing him? He totally deserved it, man."

DeVaughn's face. It got blacker than it already was. Heat waves coming off his cheeks. "You motherfucker."

Then Lafitte whispered to Melissa, "But you probably don't."

He shot her in the middle of her back and ran around the doctor's house to the backyard before anyone else knew what was going on.

Melissa crumpled to the asphalt.

DeVaughn let out a wail the likes of which this neighborhood had never heard before. He ran for her, dropped to his knees beside her.

BGMs took shots at where Lafitte had been, where they thought he had run. But he was gone. Wayward shot got DeVaughn in the shoulder. Another one got him through his other foot. He barely noticed.

The FBI man and his people dropped back into their car and screamed out in reverse. BGMs took potshots and cracked the side windows and made holes all over the front of it and the damn thing made a *clang* and some squelching and just stopped the fuck working. Cop cars finally showing up, a whole goddamn train of them. Two trains, one from each end of the street.

All the BGMs ducked into their rides and dodged cop cars that were trying to cut them off. Some made it, some didn't, the whole street a clusterfuck of cars all over lawns and the street, and sirens out of sync finally drowning out DeVaughn. People stepping out onto their porches, many with pistols in their hands. The doctor dead on his lawn, riddled with BGM bullets.

Stoudemire out of his car again, yelling into his phone

and at local cops simultaneously, the cops ignoring him, doing what they had to do—arresting BGMs and telling people to go back inside their homes and running after Lafitte and ordering some K-9s to the scene.

Then the local news van showed up.

Nobody had gotten to DeVaughn and Melissa at ground zero yet.

She was not all the way gone. Close, though. DeVaughn cradled her head and cried, *goddamn it*, and brushed hair and blood away from her mouth. The exit wound through the front of her dress had taken out her stomach and parts of her lungs and ribs, spread all across the road. She was still moving her eyes, looking up into DeVaughn's and weakly flopping her arm until her hand rested on his cheek.

"No," she said. "No."

"Baby, I'm sorry, baby. I'm so sorry, baby. I fucked up, baby. Don't leave me here, baby, baby, please, baby..."

Her rasp, critical.

She tried to say "Love." She tried again and choked and blood poured from her mouth.

He wasn't going to let her go this way. She wouldn't have wanted it that way. Fuck no. DeVaughn turned her head, let the blood fall from her mouth. He checked to make sure she was still with him. Still had a little breath in her body. Still blinking up at him, still holding her hand to his cheek.

He pulled his Glock from his waistband. Put a bullet in the chamber. "Baby."

The cops were coming closer now, guns drawn. Shouting at him but who the fuck cared?

He took Melissa's hand, wrapped it around the Glock's grip. He noticed she was maybe grinning now, the best she could do. He wasn't sure, but he hoped she had enough strength to squeeze her hand on the grip. Didn't matter. He placed her finger on the trigger. He placed the barrel in his mouth. He squeezed Melissa's finger—

Pretty sure the cops fired first. Couldn't even let a black man commit suicide the way he wanted. Had to kill him themselves. Shots fired from all around hit both Melissa and DeVaughn, but maybe Melissa had one last muscle spasm before she went away, because the Glock went off and DeVaughn's head blew open and he fell backwards as the cops kept firing.

The closest cop swore her last breath sounded something like, "Mine."

# CHAPTER THIRTY-ONE

Stoudemire said, "That was that."

Then nothing. He stayed seated, staring off at the far corner of the room, fingers absently scratching his forehead. Hospital noises in the background—beeps, blurps, barely-understandable intercom calls, cheery nurses talking to patients as if they were children. Rome waited for the punchline. It had to come. How was that an ending?

"That's...that?"

Stoudemire cleared his throat. "Yeah, sorry. Got lost in my head. Um, yeah, we got lucky. Some of the residents must have noticed what was going on outside. Called the cops, so our back-up was just in time. I think they said seven calls in three minutes. They sent an army."

"But...got 'way?"

A sigh. This guy, him and his theatrics. "We're following up on leads."

"Got...away."

"Jesus, you're going to make me say it? No, I'm not. You actually had him *in prison* and lost him, so don't even, alright?"

"Where?"

Quiet.

Rome said it again. "*Where?*"

"The dogs lost him in a Circle K parking lot. The camera was pretty old, but shows him taking off on a bike. We found the bike a week later, in the Back Bay. And we have the usual sightings. Three of them turned out to be good. Last one was in Tennessee. He's heading north again. We'll work with Minnesota's Bureau pretty closely. Except, you know, I've got to go to Washington first."

Rome shook his head. "Off the...case."

Stoudemire's expression, pissy teenager. "Not entirely."

"Yeah."

"Jesus..." Stoudemire stood. "I was sent to evaluate you, you know? See if you were in shape to help us out."

*I know.*

"The whole goddamned point of telling you, but you'd rather piss me off. You'd rather sit there in your own drool and make me look like, uh, like, like, I don't know, some sort of...you know, fuck it. I'm going to tell them you're one step above diapers. Can't even put a sentence together. No, you're not up to this."

*I know.*

"And once I tell them, it doesn't matter how many women I fuck in the line of duty, I'm still the best man for the job."

*I know.*

"Hope you get better soon, Rome." Stoudemire knuckled the plastic rail at the foot of the bed. "One day we'll get together and laugh about this. Keep your eye on the news. We'll get him."

And Stoudemire was gone.

And Rome thought: *No, you won't.*

He buzzed the nurse's station. He wanted another juice box.

\* \* \*

He kept an eye on the news. Day after day. Night after night. There was hardly anything about Lafitte at all. Some people even questioned if the havoc down South was caused by Lafitte at all. Pressure on the stepparents didn't work. They were stone cold. They gave interviews sneering at the idea they helped Billy. He hadn't seen his stepfather in ages, and it had caused a lot of bitterness. Why would they *help* that monster?

Rome wished he could take a crack at them. They had "the look." They were one thousand percent full of shit.

To catch Lafitte, an agent needed to not only think the way he did but *feel* the way he did. Lafitte was primal these days. His decisions were made by instinct, it seemed, starting with his son's death. He had lost his reason to act reasonable. Every move now was like a bug attracted to a lightbulb. Survival. Plus police training. Okay, and plus whatever the fuck he learned from Steel God. And three years in prison. Can't forget prison.

If Rome had to guess what went down in that hospital room with Ginny, it wasn't murder. But it wasn't suicide, either. It was…mercy? She had wanted to die for a long time. No one had wanted to let her. Not Rome, not her mother, not her doctors and nurses. Billy was the only one who had loved her enough to let her go. He had loved her too much to kill her, but enough to give her the means to do so.

But Lafitte had his own selfish reasons, too. Once she was dead, no one could ever use her against him again.

Survival. Bug to the bulb.

So Rome kept watching the news. He got a little

better every day. He regained control of his arms, for the most part. Still some trouble with the right side. His skull, which would be forever dented, looked less like Frankenstein's monster as the stitches came out and the scars were kind of covered as his hair grew back around them, but they were still reminders and would be for as long as he lived.

Physical therapy. Learning to keep his balance in a wheelchair, learning to push himself along. He'd probably end up in an electric wheelchair, but he would still need the ability to push himself if the battery died or he got stuck. He had to relearn how to hold his head up on his neck. It felt as if someone had a noose around it, jerking hard, but day by day it got easier. He learned to keep his spit in his mouth, to swallow again, to breathe through his nose and keep his jaw closed.

He learned to say more than two words at a time. Not complete sentences yet, but he was getting there. Maybe not next month, maybe not even next year, but eventually he would be able to *walk* into a conference room at the Bureau, even if it meant on a prosthetic leg. He would be able to *seat himself* at the table without assistance. He would be able to *give a complete statement* to the committee on why he should be retained as an independent consultant on the Lafitte case, since, obviously, Stoudemire had made an impossible mess out of the whole thing. And he would turn his much less awful face in Stoudemire's direction as he said it. He would grin while he did so. He would say, "Enough is enough. It's time to catch Lafitte, and I'm the only one who can do it."

All of them would surround him, shake his hand,

thank him for agreeing to come back. All of them except Stoudemire, of course, who would be shunned. Possibly even confined to a desk for the remainder of his career, his pay docked in order to pay for sexual harassment settlements.

It was as close to sweet dreams as Rome got anymore.

He was having one of those dreams one night—this one not in a conference room, but on a stage in front of hundreds of Special Agents, all of them honoring Rome for his diligence in pursuing Lafitte, finally catching him single-handedly on a boat in the middle of the Bering Sea as Billy tried to row to Russia.

They were calling his name. "Franklin! Franklin! Frank! Agent Rome!"

But all of their voices sounded the same, until it was one voice, not calling out loudly, but in a low rough husk.

"Rome. You there? You with me?"

He blinked awake. Room dark except for the soft nightlight above his bed, a soft blue buzz all night long. He'd become pretty good at guessing the time from the quality of light in the room and the coolness of the air and the strength of cleaning solvent. This time, two, two thirty. He turned to the voice. He would never forget that voice.

His face, though. It took looking the man in the eyes. He sat in the same chair that Stoudemire had sat in not even a month before to tell the story, but he'd moved it much closer. Knees wide, leaning forward, hands grasped together. The face, patches stretched like plastic wrap, scars like cracks in old teacups, shaved clean. His head, too, shaved clean. One ear was a bit shriveled, smaller than the other. His eyes were bright.

Rome smacked his lips a couple of time to get some moisture in his mouth. Swallowed. Then said, "Billy."

"There we go. Goddamn, man. Look at you."

Lafitte wore a white tank-T. Rome couldn't see his bottom half, but would've guessed jeans and boots. The usual. Rome looked at Lafitte's hands again to make sure he hadn't missed a knife or a gun. Billy held them up, flashed the fronts, the backs, said, "I'm clean." They were no longer wrapped in duct tape, as Stoudemire had described, but they'd definitely seen some heat. Lafitte couldn't even stretch his fingers all the way out. The skin, once again melted plastic, and too pink.

Rome then turned to the spot above him where he knew there was a camera for the nurses to watch him sleep.

"Yeah, I already got it. No one's coming. Some alone time, you and me."

Rome asked, "You okay? Your heart?"

A grin. He thumped his chest. "Could be better. Pretty sure the doc was right. It was a goddamned heart attack. It hurt like fuck, but then I got over it. The medicine helps so far. I stocked up when I got here, too." He lifted a plastic shopping back from the floor beside him, filled to the brim with pill bottles, vials, syringes, bandages, gauze, plenty more. "I got some for you, too."

Rome scrunched his eyebrows.

"Just in case."

Rome said, "Motherfucker."

Quiet.

Then Rome said, "Ginny?"

Lafitte looked away. "Feeding tube. Can't talk, can't control her arms, legs. Brain going to mush. Jesus. You got lucky, you know? You're fighting back. But Ginny, you met her. You know. I mean, she flat out *asked* me to kill her. And I couldn't. Look at her now."

"Sorry." What else to say? Even if this motherfucker was a stone cold selfish murdering pile of catshit, Rome knew what Ginny meant to Lafitte.

"Yeah. I know. Listen," Lafitte set the bag down again. "You're never going to believe me, I know, but here goes. If she hadn't shot at me first, I never would've shot her. Promise."

"Fucking liar." Rome's blood pressure monitor bleeped faster, faster.

"You tried to get me killed in prison, too. Fair is fair. Maybe we're not even, but still."

Faster, faster...

A nurse came on the intercom. "You okay in there?"

Rome stared down Lafitte hard. Said. "Fine. Bad dream."

"You sure?"

"Good. I'm fine."

He *willed* the beeping to slow down. Turned and watched the numbers go from one hundred to ninety to eighty.

Lafitte shook his head. "I figured."

"What did you figure?"

"You might hate the ever-living fuck out of me, but you're not going to let anyone else take me down. I'm all yours. Right?"

All it would take, punch the emergency call button, there was no way Lafitte could react fast enough. Rome reached for the button on the rail right next to the volume control for the TV. He'd accidentally punched it several times the last couple of months, and he knew how it worked. Loud and fast. Rubbed his thumb across it. It was *right there.*

Lafitte didn't move a muscle. The ghost of his grin still hanging right there. "Go ahead. Try it."

Rome wondered how Lafitte had gotten into the hospital without being noticed. How he had made it past all the night nurses, the security, the interns. How he had somehow disabled the camera—no, not disable. Turned it, so he wouldn't be seen. Froze it in place. So there was a chance he knew how to fuck up the call button, too. All Rome had to do was push it and find out.

If he did, this right here was over. Of course Billy would make it out. What was Rome thinking? He wouldn't have come unless he had an exit plan.

Rome pulled his thumb away from the button. Rested his hands together across his stomach. Settled back onto his pillows.

"Okay," Lafitte said. He sat up straighter. "Are you ready?"

Rome tensed, but then, why? Funny. He let his muscles go slack. He was...at peace. "Ready for what?"

Lafitte looked around the hospital room. "Aren't you tired of this place? Doesn't it smell like chemicals and death and shit? It's not doing you any good, is it?"

Rome took in a deep breath. He didn't mind it. He felt alive. "Where?"

245

"Off the grid. We'll know when we get there." Lafitte stood. "How about it?"

The call button. It was right there. *Right. There.*

Rome closed his eyes a second, thought of Desiree. First alive beside him in bed, then dead on a slab. Then he opened his eyes. It was the only shot he had.

"Okay. Let's go."

Lafitte nodded. He first switched off some of the machines at Rome's bedside, the beeping giving way to the full-on buzz of the nightlight. Dead quiet for a moment. Rome had forgotten what life sounded like without a heart monitor beeping its song at him constantly. It was sweet relief.

Billy picked up his bag of drugs, pulled the wires from Rome's arms, legs, and chest, then slid his arms under Rome's shoulders and one remaining knee, lifted him from the bed and held him close. Rome wasn't as far from the floor as he expected to be. He had forgotten how short Lafitte actually was. But he still had his strength. The man smelled the way Rome had expected him to—a dark musk that made him think of the French Quarter in summer, sitting on a barstool at the Chart Room, wondering if the bar his drink sat upon had been there since the eighteenth century.

Lafitte said, "You ready?"

Rome let out a sigh and nodded.

Maybe Rome expected an escape through the window, across the rooftops. But it wasn't like that at all.

Lafitte walked out of the room, down the hall, and through the doors to the staircase. Down three flights, then he kicked open doors and they were outside. Rome thought he heard, faintly, an alarm going off, but he could never be sure. Wishful thinking.

Parked right beside the outside door was a Honda S2000 convertible, two-seater, silver, top down.

"Nice," Rome said.

"You think?"

"Very nice."

Lafitte lowered Rome gently into the passenger seat, then hopped in himself, cranked her up and drove away as if no one was chasing them and might never chase them again.

Whatever else Rome was feeling, he sure as fuck wasn't scared. Right then, the wind chilly on his skin, his first time in a car since his ride to the airport with Wyatt, he didn't feel like his mortal enemy's hostage. He felt...free.

Finally one way or the other, they would settle this shit, mano a mano.

A few blocks away, Lafitte switched on the stereo. Some heavy metal guitar erupted, mid-song, not Lafitte's style at all. Must've come with the car. The singer was wailing, "Somebody get me a doctor!"

Rome thought, *You and me both, pal.*

Lafitte found the interstate, merged on, and headed North.

THESE TWO MOTHERFUCKERS
WILL RETURN IN
"THE SCARS OF BILLY LAFITTE"

# SPECIAL THANKS

To Allan, Kyle, and J.T., who publish the sorts of books I lust after. I am proud to be a Heathen.

To Eric Campbell at Down & Out Books for the support and reanimating my backlist. I'm proud to be one of the herd.

To Victor Gischler and Sean Doolittle, who write the sorts of books I wish I had written. I am proud to call you my closest buds.

To Rusty Barnes, Travis Neisler, and Sean O'Kane, who brutally and lovingly ripped this book apart before I showed it to anyone else, I am proud to take advice from you gents.

And especially to Brandy Smith, who makes life worth staying alive for, I am proud you married me and that you're the one I get to spend all my days and nights with.

## ABOUT THE AUTHOR

Anthony Neil Smith writes crime novels, including *Worm,
Psychosomatic, The Drummer*, the Billy Lafitte series—
*Yellow Medicine, Hogdoggin'*, and *The Baddest Ass*—and
the Mustafa & Adem series—*All the Young Warriors* and
*Once a Warrior.*

He's a Professor and the Chair of the English Department
at Southwest Minnesota State University. He likes tacos.
He likes red wine. Cheap red wine.

http://anthonyneilsmith.typepad.com.

OTHER TITLES FROM DOWN AND OUT BOOKS

*See www.DownAndOutBooks.com for complete list*

By J.L. Abramo
*Catching Water in a Net*
*Clutching at Straws*
*Counting to Infinity*
*Gravesend*
*Chasing Charlie Chan*
*Circling the Runway*
*Brooklyn Justice*

By Trey R. Barker
*2,000 Miles to Open Road*
*Road Gig: A Novella*
*Exit Blood*
*Death is Not Forever*
*No Harder Prison* (*)

By Richard Barre
*The Innocents*
*Bearing Secrets*
*Christmas Stories*
*The Ghosts of Morning*
*Blackheart Highway*
*Burning Moon*
*Echo Bay*
*Lost*

By Eric Beetner (editor)
*Unloaded*

By Eric Beetner and
JB Kohl
*Over Their Heads*

By Eric Beetner and
Frank Scalise
*The Backlist*
*The Shortlist* (*)

By G.J. Brown
*Falling* (*)

By Rob Brunet
*Stinking Rich*

By Dana Cameron (editor)
*Murder at the Beach: Bouchercon Anthology 2014*

By Mark Coggins
*No Hard Feelings*

By Tom Crowley
*Vipers Tail*
*Murder in the Slaughterhouse*

By Frank De Blase
*Pine Box for a Pin-Up*
*Busted Valentines and Other Dark Delights*
*A Cougar's Kiss* (*)

By Les Edgerton
*The Genuine, Imitation, Plastic Kidnapping*

By A.C. Frieden
*Tranquility Denied*
*The Serpent's Game*
*The Pyongyang Option* (*)

By Jack Getze
*Big Numbers*
*Big Money*
*Big Mojo*
*Big Shoes*

*(*)—Coming Soon*

OTHER TITLES FROM DOWN AND OUT BOOKS

See www.downAndOutBooks.com for complete list

By Richard Godwin
*Wrong Crowd*
*Buffalo and Sour Mash* (*)

By William Hastings (editor)
*Stray Dogs: Writing
from the Other America*

By Jeffery Hess
*Beachhead*

By Matt Hilton
*No Going Back*
*Rules of Honor*
*The Lawless Kind*
*The Devil's Anvil*

By David Housewright
*Finders Keepers*
*Full House*

By Jerry Kennealy
*Screen Test* (*)

By S.W. Lauden
*Crosswise*

By Terrence McCauley
*The Devil Dogs of Belleau Wood*

By Bill Moody
*Czechmate*
*The Man in Red Square*
*Solo Hand*
*The Death of a Tenor Man*
*The Sound of the Trumpet*
*Bird Lives!*

By Gary Phillips
*The Perpetrators*
*Scoundrels* (Editor)
*Treacherous*
*3 the Hard Way*

By Tom Pitts
*Hustle* (*)

By Robert J. Randisi
*Upon My Soul*
*Souls of the Dead*
*Envy the Dead* (*)

By Ryan Sayles
*The Subtle Art of Brutality*
*Warpath*
*Swansongs Always Begin as Love
Songs* (*)

By Anthony Neil Smith
*All the Young Warriors* (TP only)
*Once a Warrior* (TP only)
*Worm* (TP only)

By Ian Truman
*Grand Trunk and Shearer* (*)

By Lono Waiwaiole
*Wiley's Lament*
*Wiley's Shuffle*
*Wiley's Refrain*
*Dark Paradise*

By Vincent Zandri
*Moonlight Weeps*

(*)—COMING SOON

Made in the USA
San Bernardino, CA
09 December 2016